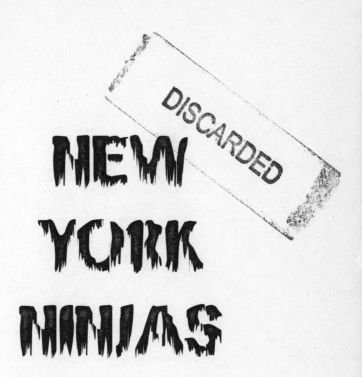

NEW YORK NINJAS

Here's what readers from around the country are saying about Johnathan Rand's *AMERICAN CHILLERS:*

"I read all of the books in the MICHIGAN CHILLERS series, and I just started the AMERICAN CHILLERS series. I really love these books!"

-Andrew K., age 13 Montana

"I have six CHILLERS books, and I have read them all three times! I hope I get more for my birthday. My sister loves them, too."

-Jaquann D., age 10, Illinois

"I just read KREEPY KLOWNS OF KALAMAZOO and it really freaked me out a lot. It was really cool!"

-Devin W., age 8, Texas

"THE MICHIGAN MEGA-MONSTERS was great! I hope you write lots more books!"

-Megan P., age 12, Kentucky

"All of my friends love your books! Will you write a book and put my name in it?"

-Michael L., age 10, Ohio

"These books are the best in the world!"

-Garrett M., age 9, Colorado

"We read your books every night. They are really scary and some of them are funny, too."

-Michael & Kristen K., Michigan

"I read THE MICHIGAN MEGA-MONSTERS in two days, and it was cool! When are you going to write one about Wisconsin?"

-John G., age 12, Wisconsin

"Johnathan Rand is my favorite author!"
-Kelly S., age 8, Michigan

"AMERICAN CHILLERS are great. I got one
for Christmas, and I loved it. Now, my sister
is reading it. When she's done, I'm going to
read it again."
-Joel F., age 13, New York

"I like the CHILLERS books because they are
fun to read. They are scary, too."
-Hannah K., age 11, Minnesota

"I read the MEGA-MONSTERS book and I
really liked it. Mr. Rand is a great writer."
-Ryan M., age 12, Arizona

"I LOVE AMERICAN CHILLERS!"
-Zachary R., age 8, Indiana

"I read your book to my little sister and
she got freaked out. I did, too!"
-Jason J., age 12, Ohio

"These books are my favorite! I love reading them!"
-Sarah N., age 10, New Jersey

"Your books are great. Please write more so I can read them.
-Dylan H., age 7, Tennessee

AMERICA'S #1 SERIES FOR MAXIMUM CHILLS!

#4: New York Ninjas

Johnathan Rand

An AudioCraft Publishing, Inc. book

Book storage and warehouses provided by Chillermania!©
Indian River, Michigan

Warehouse security provided by:
Lily Munster and Scooby-Boo

American Chillers #4: New York Ninjas
ISBN 13-digit: 978-1-893699-23-6

Librarians/Media Specialists:
PCIP/MARC records available at www.americanchillers.com

Cover illustration by Dwayne Harris
Cover layout and design by Sue Harring

Printed in USA

Dickinson Press Inc., Grand Rapids, MI USA Job # 3711700 April 2010

New
York
Ninjas

VISIT CHILLERMANIA!

WORLD HEADQUARTERS FOR BOOKS BY JOHNATHAN RAND!

Visit the HOME for books by Johnathan Rand! Featuring books, hats, shirts, bookmarks and other cool stuff not available anywhere else in the world! Plus, watch the American Chillers website for news of special events and signings at *CHILLERMANIA!* with author Johnathan Rand! Located in northern lower Michigan, on I-75! Take exit 313 . . . then south 1 mile! For more info, call (231) 238-0338. And be afraid! Be veeeery afraaaaaaiiiid . . . .

1

There are some things in this world that you just can't explain, no matter how hard you try.

This is one of those stories.

It happened to me and my friends last fall, and to make things even creepier, it happened on the scariest day of the year.

October 31st.

Halloween.

It was Friday, and I was in my bedroom doing my homework when my brother, Brad, suddenly jumped into the doorway. He was dressed in a ghost costume. I have to admit, he surprised me a little, but I wasn't about to let him know.

"Hahahaha! Gotcha!" he laughed, his arms raised up in the air. His costume was only an old white sheet with holes where his eyes were.

I shook my head and frowned. "You didn't get me at all," I said. "You look like a skinny marshmallow."

He dropped his arms. I could see his beady brown eyes staring at me through the torn holes in the sheet.

"Come on, Mike," he pleaded. "Why don't you just bag that stuff until Sunday?" He pointed to the homework on my desk.

I shook my head. "I'm going to get it done now so I don't have to worry about it all weekend," I replied.

He shrugged and left, and I returned to my homework.

That's where Brad and I are different. I'm twelve, and one year older than he is. I like to take care of things and make sure that they're done right.

Brad, on the other hand, is a little more

carefree. Oh, don't get me wrong. He's no doofus. He just likes to have his fun.

I guess we all do, now and then.

And I have to admit, I was really excited about that night.

Halloween.

My brother and I, along with Sarah Wheeler, were going to go trick-or-treating. Sarah and her family just moved into the house across the street. We live in Albany, New York, which is about one hundred and fifty miles north of New York City. That's where Sarah and her family moved from. She's becoming a good friend, and the three of us had been hanging out together.

After trick-or-treating, we were all going to go to the big Halloween party in the school gym.

We would never make it.

In just a few short hours, we would be running down sidewalks, house to house, ringing doorbells and knocking on doors.

The usual Halloween stuff.

Only, tonight would be different.

Tonight wouldn't go as planned.

Tonight, Brad, Sarah and I would find

something that would lead to the scariest night of our lives.

?.

I had just finished my homework when I heard the doorbell ring. I could hear Brad talking in the living room, and then I heard Sarah's giggle. I'd know her laugh anywhere. Sarah is the same age as Brad, only she's a little taller. And they both have the same black hair, except Sarah wears hers a lot longer.

In the next instant, there was a ghost and a witch standing at the door of my bedroom.

"Hey!" I exclaimed, admiring Sarah's costume. "That looks great!"

Her eyes grew wide, and she let out with a sharp witch cackle. It was funny, and we all laughed.

"You're not even in costume?!?!" Sarah said to me. "It's almost six o'clock!"

"He's been doing his homework," Brad sneered from beneath the white sheet.

"It'll take me ten minutes," I said. "You guys go down to the park and I'll meet you there."

They left, and I put my homework into my folder and slid it under my bed. I guess it was going to wait, after all.

Then I put my costume on. This year, I was a vampire. I made the costume myself, using one of Mom's old tablecloths as a cape. I bought a cheap Halloween make-up kit at the department store, and I made my face all white, with dark, shadowy circles around my eyes. I slicked my hair back with gel and placed a set of plastic fang-teeth in my mouth.

I stared in the mirror and smiled. I really *did* look pretty scary.

Cool.

Minutes later, I met up with Brad and Sarah at

the park.

"Mike, you look *awesome!*" Sarah shouted as I approached.

"I vant to drink your blood!" I said, wrapping my hands gently around her neck. Sarah laughed and drew away.

"Come on," Brad said from beneath his white sheet. "There are people already trick-or-treating!"

We started out. The evening sun had fallen below the trees, but it was still light out. The night was warm, too, for which I was thankful. October can be chilly in Albany, and I didn't want to have to wear a coat over my costume.

There were a lot of other kids trick-or-treating. I'm sure I knew most of them, but it was hard to recognize anyone in their costumes.

And then: disaster struck.

We had just rounded the block, when all of a sudden a dark form came from around the bushes at the corner. I tried to get out of the way — but it was too late!

The figure slammed into me, and I was sent sprawling into the bushes. Branches scratched my face, and my bag of candy went flying. I heard Sarah scream. Brad gasped.

"Hey!" Sarah shouted angrily. "Why don't you watch where you're going!?!?"

"Mike!" Brad said, scrambling to help me. I was still tangled up in the thick brush. "Are you okay?!?!"

But I wasn't paying any attention. In fact, I barely even heard him talking to me.

My attention was focused on what was partially buried beneath the dead leaves on the ground. I struggled to pull the branches away, then I swept the brittle, brown leaves aside. Now I could see the entire object.

My eyes grew.

My heart drummed.

Time stopped.

"Wow," I whispered beneath my breath.

What I had found was *incredible.*

A mask.

That's what was buried within the leaves.

But it wasn't just *any* mask. At least, it sure didn't look like any ordinary costume mask.

"Mike? Are you all right?" I heard Sarah ask. I felt a hand grasp my foot, and someone started to pull me out of the bushes.

"Hang on a second!" I said excitedly. "I found something!"

"Yeah," Brad sneered. "You found a bush. You fell into it when a big kid bumped into you."

I ignored him. I was too interested in my discovery.

The mask was dirty and stained from being in the weather. I picked it up, then struggled out of the bushes, without help from my brother.

"Check this out!" I said, scrambling to my feet. I held the mask up for Brad and Sarah to see.

"That's cool," Sarah said.

"What is it?" Brad asked.

"It's a Japanese Kabuki mask," I replied smartly.

"A *what?*" Brad asked again.

"A Japanese Kabuki mask," I repeated. "And it's *old*. It must have been in those bushes for a long time."

"How do *you* know what it is?" he asked. I could tell he thought that I was making it up.

"Because I'm older and smarter than you, that's why," I replied.

I wiped some of the dirt away from the mask. It was a reddish-gold color, but it had faded with age. The mask was heavy, and appeared to be made out of wood or some other thick material. It sure wasn't made of cheap plastic like those masks you buy at the store!

"Let me see," Sarah said.

I handed her the mask, and she held it up.

"This is cool," she said.

"Is it part of someone's Halloween costume?" Brad asked. He reached out with his ghostly arms. Sarah handed the mask to him.

"No," I replied. "Kabuki is an old form of Japanese theater. The performers use masks like these."

"I'll bet I could scare some kids with this thing!" Brad said, holding the mask up to his sheet-covered face.

"Brad, don't do that," Sarah said sharply.

"Why? Are you afraid of what I'll look like?"

"Give it back to me," I ordered, reaching out to take the mask away.

Suddenly, Brad placed the mask over his face.

"Ha ha ha!" he said, his voice muffled. "Ka-BOOOO-keee!" He held the mask to his face with one hand, then raised his free arm. "Get it? Ka-BOOOOOO-keeeeeeee!"

"Stop being a goofball!" I ordered. "Give me the mask. I'm the one who found it!"

"Ka-*BOOOOO*-keeeeee!" Brad repeated.

"Brad! Stop it!" Sarah said.

"Why?" Brad asked from behind the mask. "Am I scaring you?" He placed both hands on the side of the mask.

Then he paused.

"What the . . . ?" he said. There was a hint of panic in his voice.

"Hey!" he shouted. He was gripping the mask, trying to pry it from his face. "It's . . . it's got me! Ahhh! *I . . . I can't get it off!*"

And then he began to scream.

Brad started whirling, spinning around, his fingers grasping the mask!

"It won't come off!" he shrieked. "It . . . it won't come off!"

Sarah and I rushed to help.

"Brad! Stop!" Sarah cried. "Stop! We can help!"

Brad continued clawing at the mask over his face. Then he suddenly dove to the ground and began rolling in the grass.

"Brad!" I ordered. "Stop moving!"

In the next instant, Brad bounced back up to his feet. He had both hands on the mask, and he slowly pulled it away.

"Ha ha ha!" he snickered. "Gotcha!"

"You creep!" Sarah scolded. "You scared me!"

I snatched the mask from his hands.

"You don't know what you're doing," I said angrily. "This thing might be worth a lot of money."

"It's just a silly old mask," Brad said. "Besides—it's pretty dirty. Whoever it belongs to probably gave up looking for it before I was even born."

Brad was right. Whoever had owned the mask had probably forgotten about it long ago.

"I still think it's kind of cool," I said, handing the mask to Sarah. She held it while I picked up my bag and gathered up my Halloween candy that had spilled when I fell. Then I took the mask and gently placed it into my bag.

"Come on," Brad said, staring up into the sky. "It'll be dark soon. I want to hit the next block of houses before we call it a night."

"And the Halloween party at the school will be starting soon, too," Sarah said. "We'd better finish up our trick-or-treating or we're going to be late."

We set off—a ghost, a witch, and a vampire—bouncing from house to house, filling our bags with delicious Halloween candy and chocolate and caramel apples and other tasty treats.

Darkness seemed to come quickly that night, and soon, we were just three shadows beneath the glow of the streetlights.

Of course, we had no way of knowing it at the time, but as we made our way down the last row of houses, as we walked along the sidewalk carrying our bags of Halloween candy—

—*we were being followed!*

Sarah sensed it first.

We were just about ready to knock on the door of the last house on the street. Then, we were going to drop our candy off at our house and head for the school.

Just before I rang the doorbell, Sarah spun around.

I held my finger to the button, but I didn't press it.

"What's the matter?" I asked. Sarah was looking into the shadows on the other side of the street.

"Oh . . . I don't know," she replied. She looked around. "I just had a funny feeling, that's all. It's probably nothing."

I stared across the street. Windows in houses glowed yellow. Spiny, leafless trees fingered up into the dark night. Bushes cast spooky shadows over lawns and driveways. There were no sounds at all.

And everything seemed oddly still. There were no other trick-or-treaters, no other people outside. It was as if, for the moment, the entire city had stopped.

I was about to ring the doorbell when I heard a noise next door. It sounded like crunching leaves and branches. Brad and Sarah heard the noise, too. We all turned and peered into the bushes in the next yard.

All we could see were shadows.

"Who's there?" Brad called out.

There was no reply.

A gentle, cold breeze suddenly slithered against my cheek. A chill swept through my body, and Sarah's witch hat fell off before she could grab it. Her hair swished in the wind.

As she reached to the ground to pick up her hat, we heard the noise again.

Crunch. Ker-crunch.

We froze.

Sarah remained kneeling. Her hands grasped her hat, but she was staring off into the darkness.

"Who's there?" I demanded. "Stop trying to scare us."

"Yeah," Brad chimed in. "Come out where we can see you."

I figured that it was probably some kid hiding in the bushes. There was someone—or maybe a couple of people—hiding in the bushes, waiting to jump out and scare us.

After all . . . it *was* Halloween. That's what you do on Halloween. You try to give someone a scare.

Suddenly, the noise came again, except it was much closer now. Sarah stood up and took a step away from the bush.

Whatever it was, it was in the thick shrubbery next to the porch.

Right next to us.

"All right," I said, bravely stepping forward. "Knock it off, whoever you are."

I reached out to grab a branch. I was planning on pulling the branches away to find out who was hiding.

That's what I was *planning*, anyway.

But that's not what happened.

Because the instant I grabbed the branch was the instant that I saw the sinister, glowing eyes, glaring back at me from within the bush.

And I knew one thing for sure:

The eyes didn't belong to any prankster. They didn't belong to any costumed trick-or-treater.

Whatever was in the bushes wasn't human!

And suddenly, the creature lunged . . . *and came straight at us!*

The three of us—a witch, a ghost, and a vampire—screamed our heads off.

The creature sailed out of the bushes. I jumped out of its way and Sarah managed to escape, too . . . but the beast hit Brad square on!

"*Aaaaaaaaahhhhhh!*" Brad screamed as the creature pounced. His sheet whirled and spun as he toppled to the ground.

Suddenly, Sarah started to laugh. Then I did, too.

It wasn't a creature that had attacked . . . *it was Sarah's dog, Comet!*

"He's going to eat me!!!" Brad screeched, rolling on the ground. Fallen leaves, brown and gold, clung to his white sheet.

Sarah laughed. "No, he won't," she said. "He's just after your candy! He wants what's in your trick-or-treat bag!"

Comet is a big German Shepard. He's all black, and he looks like he can be mean.

But he's really not. Comet doesn't have a mean bone in his body.

He sure *looks* vicious, though. He gave me a scare . . . and he would probably give you a scare too!

Brad's sheet had shifted on his face, and he couldn't see. He was sure that he was being attacked by a terrible creature. His candy had spilled onto the grass and the sidewalk, and Comet was busy gulping down candy bars, chewing gum, and other treats . . . wrappers and all. He was eating so fast he was barely taking time to chew.

"Relax," I told him. "It's just Comet."

Brad got to his feet and straightened his costume, fixing his eye-holes so he could see.

"Hey, you goofy dog!" he yelled, when he saw Comet gobbling up his hard-earned treats. "That's mine! Get out of here!"

Comet didn't pay any attention—until Sarah spoke.

"Comet . . . *sit*." Her voice was calm and certain.

Instantly, the dog dropped the candy that was in his mouth and sat down, facing Sarah.

"Bad dog," Sarah scolded. Her voice was stern, but she wasn't mean.

Comet hung his head, and it was easy to see that he knew he was in trouble.

"That was not nice, Comet," Sarah continued. She leaned over and stared straight into the dog's eyes. "Go home this instant and give yourself a time out."

I know this is going to be hard to believe, but Comet slowly stood up and began to walk away, tail between his legs.

"Wow!" I said. "Did you really give him a time out?"

Sarah nodded. "Yep. He'll go home and lay down in the garage until I get home."

"Yeah," Brad snapped angrily, kneeling to pick up what was left of his Halloween candy. "He'll need some time to digest all of my stuff that he ate!"

"I'm sorry," Sarah said, bending over to help Brad. "Comet loves candy. He's usually pretty good . . . but when it comes to sweets, sometimes he just can't control himself."

When Brad had picked up the rest of his candy, he stood up.

"Man, we'd better get a move on," he said, looking up into the evening sky. "We're going to be late for the party."

But, as fate would have it, we wouldn't make it to the Halloween party.

Because there really *was* something following us.

Not a human.

Not a dog.

Something was following us.

Or, rather, some *things.*

Soon, we would know what they wanted. Soon, they would show themselves.

And that's when our night turned really ugly.

We decided to skip the last house. Instead, we would go home, drop off our Halloween candy, and meet up at a playground that's only a couple of blocks from our school.

Brad and I went to our house and dropped off our candy. I put the Kabuki mask under my bed for safe-keeping. Then I touched up my make-up. I have a pair of plastic fangs, and I popped them into my mouth, then I flashed them a few times in the mirror. I really did look pretty cool, and I thought that I might even have a chance at winning a prize in the costume contest.

I removed the fangs from my mouth and put them in my pocket. It's hard to talk with them, and I could easily slip them in when we got to the school.

Brad's sheet still had grass and leaves on it from his fall, but all he had to do was take it off, shake it a few times, and put it back on. His ghost costume was as good as new.

Ten minutes later, Brad and I were hurrying up the street toward the playground.

But something was wrong.

I couldn't put my finger on it, but something wasn't quite right . . . like when we had stopped at the door of the house, only to discover Comet lurking in the bushes.

This, however, was *different.*

All around, the night seemed dark and cold. Albany is a lot like many other cities in America. Usually, on Halloween night in Albany, you can hear the excited shrieks of kids as they tear open their Halloween candy in their homes.

Not tonight.

It had grown dark, but the streetlights burned like little blue moons. Jack-O-Lanterns glowed from porches, and Halloween decorations hung in windows. Albany is a very old city, and there are a lot of cool-looking homes that can look pretty spooky at night.

And everything was quiet.

Too quiet.

When we reached the playground, Sarah was already waiting. It was kind of funny seeing a witch sitting on a swing set!

"Hey Sarah," I began. "What do you say we—"

"*Shhhhh!*" Sarah said, pressing a single finger to her lips.

I stopped speaking. We were silent for a moment.

Then:

"*Do you hear it?*" Sarah asked quietly. She stood up from the swing.

I listened, then I shook my head. "*I don't hear a thing,*" I whispered.

"*That's what she means,*" Brad said, looking around. "*There are no sounds at all. Nothing. Not even crickets.*"

Brad was right! I knew I had sensed

something when we were walking toward the playground. I knew that the night seemed oddly quiet. But it wasn't just *quiet* . . . it was perfectly silent. Like it was . . . .

Dead quiet.

There were no sounds in the cool, night air. We heard no cars, no horns.

No crickets, no airplanes.

No laughter or kids shouting from nearby houses.

Nothing.

"Well, let's get going to the party, or we're going to be late," I said. I turned, but Sarah grabbed my arm and held it tight. I spun around.

"What?" I asked. "What is it?"

There was no answer from her. Sarah and Brad didn't move. They didn't speak. They just stood motionless, staring off into the distance. Both of their eyes were huge, like they had seen a ghost or something.

Or *something*.

And before I turned to see what they were staring at, I caught the reflection in Sarah's eyes.

No, I thought. *It can't be! It can't be!*

I whirled around and looked up into the night sky.

I gasped.

I cringed.

At that moment, there was nothing on earth that could have frightened me more.

What we saw, high in the sky, just above the trees, was—

A face.

No, not just a *face.*

A *mask.*

My mask.

The mask I had found in the bushes!

And it was huge! The mask in the sky looked like it was easily a hundred times bigger than the moon!

I was speechless. There was nothing I could say.

Nor do I think I *could* have said anything! It's kind of hard to speak when you're having the daylights scared out of you!

"Wh . . . what in the world is going on?" Brad stammered. *"That's the mask you found, Mike! That's the mask you found in the bushes!"*

"It can't be," I replied quietly. My voice trembled as I spoke. "I put it under my bed! Besides . . . the mask in the sky is huge!"

"All right," Sarah said, putting her hands on her hips. She turned and looked at me, then at Brad. "Cut the joke. What's going on? How are you doing that?"

"It's no joke," I said flatly, shaking my head. "I don't know what's happening."

The night was still very quiet, but suddenly I heard a noise. It was the padding of footsteps on pavement.

Seconds later, a giant pumpkin came into view. Not a real giant pumpkin, of course . . . but a kid wearing a costume. In fact, it was Marc DeNoyer, a kid who lives on our block. He's a little older than me, and I don't know him real well.

He saw us standing by the swings, and he walked up to us.

"You guys headed to the party?" he asked.

"Well, we were," I replied. "Until we saw *that*."

I pointed up into the air at the mask, still hanging in the night sky. Marc followed my gaze, craning his head around.

"What?" he asked. "What are you pointing at?"

"The mask," Sarah replied. She, too, raised her arm and pointed up into the sky.

"What mask?" Marc asked.

"You . . . you don't see it?" I asked.

"The only thing I see is stars and darkness."

"You don't see a Japanese Kabuki mask in the sky?" I asked.

Marc turned and looked at me. He had a strange smirk on his face, and he was shaking his head.

"You guys are weird," he stated, and he began to walk away.

"Wait!" Sarah cried. "You . . . you really don't see it?"

All Marc did was laugh and shake his head as he walked away.

"He didn't see it!" I said. "But it's there! The three of us can see it perfectly!"

We continued staring at the strange mask in the sky. It hung just above the trees, all spooky and strange.

"Maybe we're the only ones who can see it," I said. "Maybe we're the only ones who can see it because we're the ones who *found* the mask."

We were staring at the mask, not knowing what it meant, when all of a sudden . . . *its eyes began to glow!*

"Look!" I shouted. I pointed up at the mask.

Two beams of light suddenly shot down from the eyes of the mask. The beams seemed to be aimed straight down into the playground!

For the second time that evening, the three of us were paralyzed with fear.

But when we saw three dark figures appear in the beams of light, we knew that the real trouble was about to begin.

"Okay," Brad whispered. *"Now I'm really freaked. Let's get out of here!"*

"Wait," Sarah said. *"Let's see what they are."*

I wasn't sure I wanted to hang around, but I felt better with Brad and Sarah there. If I had been alone, I would have split a long time ago!

The three forms stood motionless in the park. They were too far away to see who—or *what*—they were.

Suddenly, the mask in they sky began to fade. It went dimmer and dimmer until it just slipped into the dark night.

But below, on the far side of the playground, the three figures stood. Three dark, shadowy figures below a single streetlight. They were clothed from head to toe in dark linen, like they were wearing black robes.

"Who do you think they are?" I asked quietly.

"Well, I'll bet they're not the Three Stooges," Brad replied.

What happened next is hard to explain.

Without warning, the three figures began to move.

Which isn't so strange. It was the *way* they moved that freaked us out!

The three figures began to whirl and flip! One of them flipped over and over in a series of handsprings. In seconds they had vanished into the shadows between the houses.

"Did you see that?!?!?" Brad exclaimed from beneath his ghost sheet. "That was weird! They were like . . . like acrobats!"

"Yeah," Sarah agreed. "Halloween acrobats from a creepy carnival."

I shook my head, but I didn't say anything. My eyes darted from one side of the street to the other, looking for any sign of the three mysterious figures.

"Ah, it was probably just three people in their Halloween costumes," I said. "We'll probably see them at the Halloween party at the school."

Brad glared at me.

"Mike, you saw the same things we did! The mask in the sky, the beams of light! You saw that, too!"

Brad was right. What we saw was no prank. It was no Halloween trick.

We just couldn't explain it, that's all.

And now we had another problem.

To get to the school, we had to walk right past the place where the three strange figures had appeared. There was no other way, unless we wanted to turn around and go all the way around the other block, up another street, and then around another couple blocks.

"I think they're gone," Sarah said, adjusting her witch hat. She looked at us. "Come on."

She began walking, and Brad and I followed. I have to admit I wasn't too sure about this. I was really confused and a bit freaked out by what we had seen.

Halloween pranksters, I told myself. *That's all they were. Three people in Halloween costumes. We'll probably see them at the school party.*

But I didn't have a good feeling about it.

As we walked, the three of us peered into dark shadows and murky corners, searching for any sign of the three strange figures. We saw nothing.

Until Brad suddenly stopped, turned, and froze. He grabbed Sarah by the arm, and she stopped, too.

And when I saw what he was staring at, I thought I was going to faint right then and there.

A shadow.

No, not just a shadow.

The shadow of someone, lurking in the darkness near a house. The figure was hard to make out, but it there was no mistaking it: the figure was a human.

We all stared. I could feel the hair on my head beginning to rise. My skin grew cold.

And then:

The figure moved. It slunk along the side of the house, like it was trying not to be seen. Then it turned around the corner of the house and vanished.

"Do . . . do you think he's seen us?" Brad asked.

"I shook my head. "I don't think so," I replied. "Whoever it is, they look like they're trying to hide from someone."

"Or sneak up on someone," Sarah suggested. "Come on." She began tip-toeing across the grass.

"What are you doing!?!?" I hissed. *"Sarah! What are you doing?!?!"*

Sarah stopped and turned. I couldn't see her face; only the silhouette of her witch costume. "I want to know what's going on," she replied. "This is our neighborhood. It's up to us to know what's going on. Come on."

Sarah was right, I guess. If there was something going on that shouldn't be, we could call the police.

But I still wasn't sure about sneaking around the house to investigate the dark figure we had spotted.

Besides . . . there had been three dark figures a few minutes ago. Three figures that had appeared in beams of light from a mask high in the sky.

And so, I followed Sarah across the lawn. Brad followed a step behind me.

"*I don't like this,*" he said softly. "*I don't like this at all.*"

"*It's nothing,*" I said confidently. "*It's just someone in a Halloween costume.*"

In seconds, we had arrived at the corner of the house. Sarah peered around the side and I leaned over her shoulder. Brad kneeled in the soft grass and peeked around my leg, and the three of us stared into the shadowy backyard.

There was nothing to see, other than the normal, everyday things that you would see in a backyard in Albany: a teeter-totter, a picnic table, a few small trees. It was hard to see in the darkness, but we could make out the forms in the dim glow of the streetlight that came from the other side of the house.

But there was no sign of the figure we had spotted sneaking alongside the house.

"*He's gone,*" I whispered.

I relaxed and stood up, and so did Brad. Sarah continued peering around the corner.

"Well, whoever it was, they took off," she said.

"Let's go," Brad said in frustration. "We're already late for the school Halloween party. I don't want to miss the costume contest." He raised his arms and his sheet spread out. "Oooooooooo," he said. "We'll have a haunting good time."

I laughed, and so did Sarah. Sometimes Brad can be pretty funny.

We turned and were about to walk across the lawn and back to the sidewalk . . . but it was going to be impossible.

Because the dark figure was only a few feet from us, blocking our way.

Oh no! While we were trying to sneak up on him, he had been sneaking up on us!

11

Sarah screamed.

Brad screamed.

I gasped, and I tried to run. Instantly, I was stopped by a large hand that grasped my shoulder. Sarah tried to run, but she, too, was stopped. Her witch hat fell from her head, but she caught it in her hands. Brad stood his ground, unmoving. I think he was too afraid to do anything.

"Caught you, you little tricksters!" a gruff voice said. "Caught you red-handed!"

I managed to wriggle free, and I stepped back.

Sarah did, too, and the three of us stared at the large, dark figure that loomed over us.

"Thought you were going to get away, didn't you?" the man said.

I was shaking in my shoes, but I managed to speak.

"Get away from who?" I asked.

"Oh, you know perfectly well," the man said. "You three are the ones that have been toilet-papering the trees around my house!"

"What?!?!?" Sarah exclaimed. She placed her pointed black hat on her head. "We haven't done any such thing! We were on our way to a Halloween party!"

"Come over here so I can see you," the man huffed.

We followed him along the side of the house and into his driveway. The streetlight lit up the yard and the front of the house, and now I could see the man's features. He was about my dad's age, and he had a mustache.

But it was then that I noticed several trees in his yard. White streams of toilet paper streaked the trees. Someone had made an awful mess.

"So, where are you hiding them?" the man demanded.

"Hiding what?" I asked. I didn't know what he was talking about.

"The toilet paper rolls," he said angrily, extending an open palm. "Hand them over, and then I'm going to call your parents. I might even call the police."

The police! But . . . we hadn't done anything!

"Look," Sarah said, raising her arms out for him to see. "Where would we hide rolls of toilet paper? We aren't the ones you're looking for. We're on our way to school to go to a Halloween party."

The man looked at Sarah, then to Brad, then to me. Brad raised his sheet from around himself. Beneath his costume, he wore blue jeans and a gray sweatshirt. It was plain to see that he wasn't hiding any toilet paper.

"It's true," I said, nodding. "We didn't do any of this." I gestured toward the vandalized trees. "We don't do things like this. Honest."

I wasn't sure if he believed me or not, and I knew that we would be in big trouble if we couldn't convince him of the truth. I wouldn't even think of toilet papering someone's trees. I mean . . . I like to play jokes and pranks now and then, but I wouldn't do anything that would get me into trouble.

And neither would Sarah or Brad.

Suddenly, I caught a movement across the street. Sarah saw it, too, and her eyes grew wide. She pointed.

"Look!" she exclaimed.

Across the street, in the darkness, two dark shadows had emerged. They appeared to be kids, maybe a couple of years older than us.

And we could see rolls of toilet paper in their hands!

"Hey you kids!" the man suddenly boomed. His voice echoed up and down the block. "Hold it right there!"

The two kids froze, and the man charged across the street.

"Let's get out of here!" Brad exclaimed, and the three of us wasted no time scurrying to the sidewalk and running up the street. Behind us, we could hear the man bawling out the two kids.

"Man, I'm glad we got out of that one!" I said.

"Yeah," said Sarah. "We would've been in big trouble for something we didn't even do!"

But I didn't say anything. As we walked, my mind drifted back to the mask we had found — the same strange mask that the three of us had seen in the sky.

And the three figures that had suddenly appeared. Who were they? Where had they gone?

Something told me that there was more to this than I could imagine. Something that would mean big, big trouble.

And when we rounded the last block before reaching the school and saw the three hooded figures standing directly in our path, I knew that I had been right.

We were in big, big trouble.

Now, I know this is going to sound unbelievable, and I wouldn't blame anyone if they thought that I was making this up.

But I knew right then and there what we were seeing.

Ninjas.

That's right.

Ninjas, dressed all in black, wearing dark hoods over their heads and faces. I was certain that the three figures that we now saw were the same figures that had mysteriously appeared in the playground.

Sarah, Brad, and I stopped in our tracks. The three of us—a witch, a ghost, and a vampire—gasped at the same time.

The three dark figures seemed to stare at us, motionless. They were in a fighting stance, but they didn't flinch a muscle.

"G . . . goo . . good c-c-costumes, guys," Brad managed to stammer. His voice was filled with fear.

The three ninjas didn't respond. They didn't say a word, didn't move an inch.

"Well, uh . . . hey," I said. "Nice seeing you." I backed up a step. "We gotta run. See ya later."

Sarah, Brad, and I made a wide circle around the three figures. Our eyes never left the dark forms on the sidewalk.

As we walked around them, their gaze followed, and they turned their heads and changed their stance so they could watch us.

But they didn't come after us. They remained right where they stood, watching *us* watching *them*.

"*Let's get to the school,*" Sarah whispered. "*Those guys are freaky.*"

We walked quickly along the sidewalk, each of us snapping our heads around to see the three ninjas still poised in place. They seemed to be watching us walk away.

Brad turned to look one last time, and then stopped walking.

"They're gone!" he exclaimed.

Sarah and I stopped and turned. The three figures were nowhere in sight.

"I don't know what they were trying to do," I said. "But if they're trying to creep me out, it worked. I'm glad we got away from them."

The three of us turned to continue walking to the school . . . but we didn't even get a chance to take a single step.

Because the ninjas had returned!

Somehow, they were now *in front of us!* I know it was impossible, but there they were . . . *right in front of us!*

And something told me that, this time, getting away from them wasn't going to be so easy.

This time, we didn't even try to move. We were shocked that, somehow, someway, the three ninjas had been able to get in front of us so quickly, and without us even seeing them.

Impossible!

But there they were. Right in front of us, in fighting stance, ready for battle.

Suddenly, their eyes began to glow!

From behind their dark veils, their eyes began to glow a ghostly yellow, like candles.

We were more than simply freaked out.

We were *horrified.*

How strange a sight this must be, if anyone else had been watching at that very moment! A witch, a ghost, and a vampire—confronted by three black ninjas with glowing eyes!

But . . . .

Could the ninjas just be people in Halloween costumes? I've seen some pretty far-out costumes, and I imagined that it might be possible that the three figures we were staring at might just be three people in really good costumes.

"Who . . . who are you?" I said, my voice cracking.

The three hooded figures didn't reply. They stood their ground, eyes glowing yellow, a fire burning from behind their dark veils.

"I don't like this," Brad whispered. *"I don't like this one bit."*

Suddenly, Sarah spoke up. She was angry.

"Leave us alone!" she demanded. "Leave us this instant! Right now!"

That was all it took! Without any hesitation, the three ninjas began to move!

At first, it was like they were moving in slow motion. Then, they began to whirl and twirl and twist and turn. They fled, one of them flipping end-over-end in sharp hand-springs, another spinning and churning like a top. Each went in a different direction, disappearing into the shadows of the night.

"Wow," Brad said to Sarah. "I guess you really showed them!"

Sarah stood proudly, looking into the shadows for any sign of the strange ninjas.

"That'll teach them to mess with you!" I said.

But I spoke too soon.

Just then, I heard a noise from behind us. We whirled, and for the umpteeth time that night, I felt the blood rush from my face.

And now, I realized that Sarah hadn't been the one to scare away the ninjas.

They had been scared off by the mysterious, wisping form that was right behind us!

Right in front of us, only a few feet away, a strange white fog whirled.

"What . . . what's going on?" I stammered, backing away. Brad and Sarah took a few steps back, too. The three of us watched, our mouths open wide.

Suddenly, there was a figure standing in the fog! He looked identical to the three ninjas we had seen only moments before, only this one was dressed all in white. His arms were crossed, and his feet were apart.

What a bizarre night this was turning out to be!

"Something tells me this isn't the Pillsbury Doughboy," Brad whispered.

I elbowed him in the ribs.

"This isn't a time for jokes," I said quietly.

The three of us just stood there, watching the figure watching us. The fog disappeared, and the strange form simply stood on the sidewalk, bathed in the light from the street lamp above.

And then, from behind us:

Footsteps.

"Hey guys! What's up?"

I whirled to see—

A werewolf!

Well, not a real werewolf, of course. It was a werewolf costume, and his voice sounded just like Kyle Stryker, one of our classmates.

He came up to us and stopped.

"Headed to the school party?" he asked.

The three of us said nothing. I responded by pointing my thumb in the direction of the white ninja.

"Awesome costume, dude!" Kyle the

werewolf exclaimed. "Man . . . that sure looks real!"

"I don't think it's a costume," I replied. "I think that he's real."

"Get outta here!" Kyle replied. He burst forward and stepped up to the ninja.

"Who's in there?" he said, leaning toward the white figure. Kyle's head swayed back and forth, like he was trying to see within the costume.

"I know who you are!" he suddenly exclaimed. "You're Mr. Helms!"

Mr. Helms is a teacher at our school. In fact, he was my teacher last year.

But the white figure in front of us was too short to be Mr. Helms, I was sure of it.

And besides . . . Mr. Helms couldn't just magically appear like this guy had!

"That's who you are!" Kyle said loudly. "It sure is a great costume, Mr. Helms!"

Kyle the werewolf walked around the hooded ninja, inspecting his costume.

"Come on," Kyle urged. "Take off your mask."

The white ninja remained motionless.

"Well, if you don't take off that mask, I will," Kyle stated. He reached his hand toward the ninja's face.

"Kyle! Don't!" Sarah ordered. "I don't think it's Mr. Helms! I think—"

But it was too late. Kyle had grasped part of the white hood, and yanked it up and off the figure.

We all knew instantly that Kyle had done the worst thing he could have possibly done. He had thought that when he pulled the hood off, he would see the face of Mr. Helms smiling back at him.

Of course, what he saw *definitely* wasn't Mr. Helms.

I gasped.

Brad let out a kind of choking sound as his breath went away.

Sarah's hands flew to her face, covering her mouth.

And Kyle screamed.

The white ninja had no head!

When Kyle had yanked the hood from the figure, we all had expected to see the face of someone. True, I didn't expect it to be Mr. Helms.

But I didn't expect the figure to have no head at all!

Stunned, Kyle dropped the hood on the sidewalk. Instantly, he spun and sped past us, shrieking all the way down the street. We could still hear him screaming as he rounded the corner and fled down the next block.

I was thinking that maybe we should have done the same thing. I didn't have a good feeling about some headless white ninja standing right in front of me!

"Let's get out of here!" Brad hissed.

We were about to turn and run when suddenly, the white ninja moved! He bent down swiftly, picked up his hood, and placed it back over his . . . well . . . the place where his head should be.

And he spoke!

His voice was old and creaky, like it was difficult for him to talk.

"Do not be alarmed, children," he said. "I know that you must be confused."

Confused? I thought. *That has got to be the understatement of the year!*

"Please let me explain. We do not have much time left, and my time here is short. Tell me . . . which one of you has found the mask?"

I pointed at Brad, and Brad pointed at me.

"He did!" we both said at the same time.

The ninja nodded toward Brad, then toward me. I tried to see behind his veil, but all I could see were black holes where his eyes should have been.

"I . . . I was the one to find it," I confessed. "But I didn't steal it or anything! I found it in the bushes. I didn't even know—"

The white ninja raised his arm, showing a hand wrapped in cloth. I stopped speaking.

"There is no need for you to explain," he said. "It is I who must explain. That is what I am here to do."

I don't know what he thought he was going to explain. How could anyone possibly explain a headless white ninja, on Halloween night in Albany, New York?

"Are . . . you . . . are you like . . . a ghost or something?" Brad asked.

"It is not important who I am," the white ninja replied. "What is important is my message, and what I have to say to you. Now that you have found the mask, there isn't much time left."

He had said that before, that there *'wasn't much time left.'* I wondered what he meant.

He took a step toward me.

"So," he said. "You are the one? The one who

touched the mask first?"

"I didn't break it, honest! I'll give it to you, if—"

"No," he interrupted. "It is not the mask that I want. It is what needs to be done *with* the mask that matters."

By this time, I had already figured that we weren't going to make it to the school Halloween party. I knew that by now, it was already too late, and that we'd miss all of the fun activities and costume contest.

But when the white ninja told me what the mask was all about, I wasn't worried about the party anymore. I wasn't worried about winning a prize or even seeing my friends in their costumes.

Because what the white ninja said made me wonder if the three of us would even survive the night.

"The mask that you have found is the ancient Mask of the Masters," the white ninja said. "It is a mask created by a powerful ninja, many years ago. Its power is legendary."

"I told you that you should have left it in the bushes," Brad whispered.

"You did not!" I shot back quietly. *"You didn't tell me any such thing!"*

"The Mask of the Masters was stolen by the dark ninjas. They wanted to use its power for their awful deeds. However, it was stolen once again . . . this time by thieves who wished to sell it for a fortune."

"But who did the mask belong to in the first place?" I asked.

"Ah, yes," the white ninja said. "Thousands of years ago, in a land far away, it was created by a great ninja king. He created it . . . and its powers . . . and gave it to his daughter as a gift. She was a warrior princess. A great ninja in her own right.

"But it was stolen by the dark ninjas before he gave it to her. Since then, it has been stolen and sold many times. Finally, it became the property of a museum . . . where it was stolen once again. But the thieves became afraid when strange things began to happen. This is what is known as the 'curse' of the mask. Whoever this curse falls upon will have terrible nightmares for the rest of their life. There will be no rest, no escape from the awful dreams."

"That would be terrible!" Sarah exclaimed.

"One of the robbers," the white ninja continued, "in a desperate attempt to get rid of the mask and the curse, threw it out of a car window. Since then it has remained hidden . . . until today."

"You mean . . . when I found it?" I said.

"Yes," his old voice creaked. "Until you found it. But now, we have a chance to rid those who wish to use the mask for their own wickedness. We have a chance to stop them."

"You mean those three dudes that we saw earlier?" Brad asked.

"Precisely," the white ninja replied. "It is good that you have it, though. It would be a terrible thing if the Mask of the Masters fell into the hands of the dark ninjas."

Oh no! The mask! I left it under my bed in my room!

My heart sank. A boulder wedged in my throat.

"The mask!" I exclaimed. *"It's under my bed! It's under my bed at my house!"*

Although I couldn't see his face, the white ninja appeared to be shocked.

"You must get the mask and keep it with you. The mask has special powers to protect itself, but those powers alone aren't strong enough to stop the dark ninjas from stealing it again! The Mask of the Masters must remain with you at all times until you take it to the sacred ground! Then, the great battle can begin."

"Sacred ground?!?!?" Brad said. "Great battle?!?! What are you talking about?"

"Whoever finds the mask has only four hours to take it to the sacred ninja ground. It must be taken there, or —"

His voice faded, and I waited for him to finish.

"Or else what?" I asked.

"Or else whoever found the mask will have the curse of the dark ninja upon them for the rest of their life."

Gulp! The thought of having nightmares every single night for the rest of my life freaked me out!

"Just where did you come from?" Brad asked. "Are you like . . . a ghost or something?"

"There is no time for me to explain further," he continued. "You must find the mask. Get the mask and take it to the sacred ground. I cannot stay any longer. You *must* get the mask! I don't care what you have to do. Take it to the sacred ground! Hurry!"

"But where is the sacred ground?!?" I asked.

"I will send you a clue," the white ninja replied. "Please . . . you must hurry!"

And with that, the white ninja simply

vanished. His body seemed to go blurry, and then turn a very bright white.

Then he was gone.

"What in the world is going on?!?!" Brad said.

"I don't know," I replied. "But we'd better do as he says. I don't want to have a ninja curse for the rest of my life! Come on. We've got to get that mask."

We started to run along the sidewalk.

"What did he mean by 'four hours'?" Brad huffed as he ran.

"I don't have a clue," I said. "But if I only have four hours to take it somewhere, then we're already short of time. I found that mask over two hours ago!"

The three of us paced along the sidewalk, running frantically. Our house was only a few blocks away, and when we rounded the next block, we'd be able to see our porch light.

Except—

We weren't going to make it around the corner.

Because a large, dark figure suddenly leapt out from the shadows and stood on the sidewalk, blocking our way home.

It was all I could do to stop myself before running into the large, dark shape that suddenly appeared before us.

Instantly, I was seized by a powerful arm. Brad was, too.

"And where do you think you punks are going?" I heard a husky voice say.

And I knew who it was. That voice belonged to the biggest bully on the block, Cully McGinty. He's fifteen, and he's nothing but a trouble maker.

"I don't think you heard me," he said, shaking my collar. "I asked you a question, twerp."

"It's none of your business!" I barked, trying to twist out of his grasp.

"Oh, yes it is," he said. "I want your Halloween candy. Give it to me."

"We don't have any!" Sarah snapped. "Let them go!"

"I wasn't talking to you, witch," Cully said.

"We don't have any candy!" Brad said. Cully had a handful of white sheet, and Brad struggled to get away. It was useless.

"We were going to a Halloween party," I insisted. "We don't have any candy!"

"Let them go!" Sarah demanded. "Right now!"

"Tsk, tsk, the little witch is mad," Cully mocked. "What are you going to do, little witchy-poo? Cast a spell on me? Turn me into a frog?"

I twisted and turned, but it was no use. Cully was strong, and he held tightly to the cape around my neck. I wasn't going anywhere.

What happened next isn't all that clear. There was a sudden flurry of movement, a blur of arms and legs. In the next breath, Cully was on the ground, flat on his back. Brad and I were still standing, and Sarah was at our side.

"Run!" Sarah exclaimed, and the three of us bolted down the street.

"I'm going to get you punks for that!" I could hear Cully shout from behind us. "You're going to be sorry for that, witch! I'm going to get you!"

Sarah managed to laugh as the three of us sprinted down the street.

"What did you do to him?" I asked as I ran. My black shoes smacked against the pavement.

"Oh, it was just a trick my older brother taught me," Sarah replied, huffing and puffing. " He had both of his hands on you guys. I was able to trip him and knock him off balance before he could do anything!"

"Great," Brad said. "Now we're going to have Cully McGinty after us . . . plus those three creepy ninjas."

Up ahead, I could see lights on in my house. Relief welled up inside me . . . until I saw the dark shadow through my bedroom window.

Oh no! We were too late! The three dark ninjas had discovered where I'd hidden the mask!

I stopped at the curb and pointed.

"Look!" I exclaimed, thrusting my finger in the direction of my bedroom window. "We're too late!"

Brad and Sarah stopped running and looked where I was pointing. There were no lights on in my bedroom, but I could see the dark shape of someone moving around inside.

Then another figure moved!

I couldn't believe that the three ninjas were in my bedroom! If only I had known that the mask was more than just an ordinary mask! I would have never left it under my bed.

But then I had another thought.

A terrible thought.

An *awful* thought.

If the three ninjas were in my house, then what about Mom and Dad? What had happened to them?!?!?

I couldn't wait a moment longer.

"Let's go!" I shouted, and sprang across the lawn.

"*Mike!*" Brad shouted. "*Where in the world are you going?!?!?*"

"*Inside!*" I said. "*Come on! We have to stop them! We have to help Mom and Dad!*"

I bolted onto the porch with Sarah and Brad close behind. My hand found the doorknob and I pushed the door open and burst inside.

In the living room, the television was on. A newspaper was spread out on the couch, and a half-filled glass of iced-tea sat on a coffee table.

"*Mom!*" I shouted. "*Dad!*"

I ran across the living room. "*Mom! Dad!*"

"Where could they be?" Sarah asked.

I began to think the worst. I began to think

that something terrible had happened. After all, if those three ninja warriors wanted the mask, there probably wasn't much Mom or Dad could do to stop them.

And then I wondered something else.

Maybe I'm wrong, I thought. *Maybe the shadows in my bedroom weren't ninjas at all. Maybe it was only Mom and Dad.*

I turned to walk down the hall and stopped dead in my tracks.

A surge of terror thundered through my entire body.

Behind me, I heard Sarah and Brad gasp.

Because right in front of me, coming out of my bedroom, was a ninja! He was dressed in all black, with a veil covering his face.

And he was carrying a sword!

I jumped back and screamed like I had never screamed before. Sarah and Brad screamed.

I spun on my heels and the three of us ran back into the living room, heading for the front door. We were getting out of there!

"Stop!!!" the dark ninja ordered.

At least . . . it was the ninja that had spoken . . . but it was the voice of—

"What on earth is going on?!?!"

—my dad?!?!?!

I was just about to burst out the front door, but the voice caused me to stop. I spun, just as the ninja came around the corner. He reached his hand up and pulled off his veil.

Dad! It was just my dad, after all! And, now that I had a closer look, he didn't look all that threatening. His ninja costume looked a little silly, actually. He was wearing an old black bathrobe and dress socks that went up to his knees.

"What in the world is going on?!?!" he demanded.

Just then, Mom came around the corner of the hall . . . only she was dressed like a nurse! Which was strange, because Mom isn't a nurse. She teaches at a college.

"I thought that . . . I mean, you . . . you look like a ninja," I replied. "Well, sort of, anyway."

"Of course I do. Your mother and I are going to a Halloween party on the next block."

"But . . . you're dressed as a ninja," Brad said.

"Yeah," Dad said proudly. "What do you think?" He raised his sword, which I now recognized as an old plastic toy sword that I'd had for a long time. I didn't play with it anymore, and I'd even forgotten that it was still in my closet.

"I had the hardest time trying to figure out what to be," he said. "Then I saw these three guys running down the block in ninja costumes. That gave me an idea. I just used this old bathrobe and some black socks, and I made this veil out of a piece of old black cloth." He placed it over his head.

Now that I had a closer look, Dad didn't look like much of a ninja at all. I couldn't believe he was actually going to leave the house wearing that outfit. He really looked goofy.

"Wait a minute," Sarah said. "Did you say that you saw three ninjas outside?"

Dad nodded. "They sure looked great. I mean, their costumes were really awesome."

"Dad, they weren't wearing costumes!" I explained. "They were actual ninjas! *Real* ninjas, Dad!"

Mom laughed, and Dad shook his head. "Okay, what's the joke?" he replied.

"It's no joke," Brad chimed in. "There are three ninjas running around. *We* saw them, too!"

I told Mom and Dad about the mask that I had found. I told them it was very old and had strange powers. I explained about the white ninja that had appeared and told us we only had a short time left to return the mask to sacred ground.

Dad listened, grinning all the while. I knew that he didn't believe me.

"All right," I said. "I'll prove it."

I walked through the living room past Mom and Dad, and walked down the hall.

"Come here and I'll show you."

Mom and Dad followed me. Behind them, Sarah and Brad followed, too.

I fell to my knees and reached under my bed.

"I'll prove it," I said, reaching for the mask. "I have the mask right —"

I stopped speaking.

My hands had found nothing. There was nothing beneath my bed!

The mask was gone!

21

I fell to the floor and pressed my cheek against the carpet.

There was nothing beneath my bed, except for a few dust kitties and an old sock near the wall.

I was flabbergasted.

"It . . . it was right here!" I stammered. *"I put it right here, under my bed!"*

I stood up. Mom and Dad were smiling. Sarah and Brad had a look of shock upon their faces.

"Well, if you find it, let us know," Mom said. "Maybe you can conjure up those ninjas again and get your father a better costume.

They didn't believe me!

"I'm serious!" I said.

"And we're *late*," Dad replied, looking at his wristwatch. "It's already seven-thirty. We'll be home in an hour or so." He turned and walked out of my bedroom. Mom followed.

Sarah walked over to my bed and peered down.

"Are you serious?" she asked. "Is the mask really gone?"

I nodded. "I don't understand. I put it right here for safe-keeping."

"Now what do we do?" Brad replied.

Sarah adjusted her pointed witch hat and then put her hands on her hips. "We have to find that white ninja again, and tell him what happened."

"But how do we find him?" I asked. "How do we know where he is? He didn't even tell us where to find him after we'd retrieved the mask. Maybe he'll just magically appear somewhere."

I heard the front door open and close. I looked out my bedroom window and saw Mom and Dad walking down the driveway to the sidewalk.

I laughed out loud. Mom's nurse costume looked pretty good, but *Dad* . . . now that was a different story altogether. He looked really silly in his home-made ninja outfit.

Sarah laughed, too. "With that robe on, he looks like he just got out of bed!" she giggled.

But Brad wasn't laughing. He wasn't smiling. He was looking up at the ceiling, his face twisted with shock and surprise.

"*Look!*" he exclaimed.

Sarah and I followed his gaze to the ceiling, and neither of us could believe what we saw.

It was the mask!

Above us, the mask hung flat against the ceiling, like it had been glued there.

"How did . . . " My voice faded, and I didn't finish my sentence.

The three of us just stared, dumbfounded, at the mask on the ceiling. I had no idea how it got there.

And if *that* wasn't strange enough, all of a sudden the mask began to *shake!* It shivered and trembled, vibrating on the ceiling. As it did, we watched as it slowly began to lower.

The mask was floating in the air! It was floating all by itself!

"Okay," Brad said. His voice shook as he spoke. "I'm spooked. I'm really, really spooked. Like . . . this *isn't* normal." He backed up and stood in the doorway.

Above us, the mask continued to come down. Slowly, very slowly, it descended from above, like it was as light as a feather.

I held my hands out, and the mask gently settled into my palms. I could feel its smoothness, feel its weight in my hands.

"Wow!" I exclaimed. *"This is too freaky!"*

"Let's go," Sarah urged. "We have to find that white ninja guy and find out what we're supposed to do with this thing."

Sarah was right. The white ninja had been serious.

"But he said he would send us a clue," I said. "I wonder what he meant by a clue?"

"I don't know," Sarah replied. "But maybe we could find him again."

Problem was, where would we find him? What did he want us to do with the mask? He had said something about taking it to some 'sacred ground' or something. But what did he mean by that? Where was this 'sacred ground'? What kind of clue would we receive, if we received any clue at all?

And, more importantly, how much time did we really have left before it was too late?

Questions snarled in my head like a swarm of bees. I didn't have an answer to any of them.

"Well, I suppose we could take it back to the place where the white ninja appeared," I said. "I guess that's as good of a place as any."

I looked at the mask in my hand, and turned it over. It was hard to believe that it was so old and powerful.

Brad turned and walked down the hall. Sarah and I followed, and soon, we were outside, walking down the sidewalk on our way back toward the place where the white ninja had appeared. As I walked, I held the mask tightly with both hands. There was no way I was going to let it get out of my sight!

Houses along the street were lit up. Most of them were decorated with Halloween things like cats and witches and jack-o-lanterns. Carved pumpkins glowed on porches. Above, stars twinkled like tiny, frozen fireflies.

We reached the place where the white ninja had appeared.

"Well?" Brad asked, looking around. "What now?"

"I don't know," I said, peering into shadows and around dark corners. Laughter came from one of the houses. Inside, I could see the shapes of people in a variety of costumes. I imagined that lots of people were having their own Halloween parties.

"I wonder where he is?" Sarah said.

We were shocked when, all of a sudden, a voice answered from the bushes.

"Right here," the voice said.

Suddenly, without warning, a pair of arms reached out from within the branches. It happened so fast that there was nothing I could do.

In a split-second the outstretched arms had reached around the mask that I held in my hands. Instantly the mask was pulled away, and the arms disappeared back into the bushes.

The mask was gone!

Someone . . . or something . . . had been hiding in the bushes, and now they had taken the mask!

Without even thinking about it I reached out and pulled the branches away. I was a little afraid, but I couldn't worry about that now. The only thing I knew was that I had to have that mask back.

"Hey!" I shouted as I pulled the thick branches apart. I peered in the shadowy darkness, looking for whoever had taken my mask.

Suddenly, a dark form moved right in front of

me!

I took a step back and so did Brad and Sarah—just as Cully McGinty emerged from the bushes.

And he was holding my mask!

"Looking for something, shrimp?" he taunted, waving the mask above his head.

"That doesn't belong to you!" I shouted. "Give that back!"

"Awww . . . little vampire is mad," he mocked. "Please don't bite my neck little vampire!"

He was making fun of me!

Sarah spoke up. "You'd better give that mask back or you're really going to be in for it!"

"Pipe down, witchy-poo," Cully snapped. "I owe you one, anyway. Besides . . . I *like* this mask." He flipped it up in the air, and caught it. "It looks cool. I think I'm going to keep it and hang it on my bedroom wall."

"Cully, you don't know what you're doing," I said harshly. "I really need to have that back. Besides . . . it doesn't belong to you."

"Hey, I found it," he said innocently.

"You *swiped* it!" Brad shot back from beneath his ghost costume.

"Quiet, you over-sized foam cup," Cully replied, "or I'll yank that sheet off of you and tie you up in it!"

Brad didn't say anything more. He didn't want to get into a fight with Cully. I don't think any of us did.

"See you punks later!" Cully exclaimed, and with that, he began running down the street, the Japanese Kabuki mask tucked beneath his arm.

The three of us stood on the sidewalk, not sure what to do. My heart was racing.

And I was *angry*, too. That mask didn't belong to Cully.

Actually, it didn't belong to me, either. All I knew was that I had to take it to some sacred ground that the white ninja guy had told us about.

But if I didn't get that mask back from Cully, it would be too late.

"Come on!" I shouted. *"We have to get that mask back!"* I started to run after Cully.

Brad and Sarah snapped into action. Sarah had to pull off her hat and carry it in her hand to keep it from flying away.

"What are we going to do if we catch him?!?!" Brad shouted from behind me.

"We'll think about that later!" I replied.

Our feet drummed the sidewalk. Up ahead, rounding the block, I could see the dark shadow of Cully McGinty. He was still running fast. Then, he disappeared around the corner.

"We have to catch up to him!" I said. *"We have to get that mask back!"*

The three of us were just rounding the corner beneath a street light, when I heard an awful, unearthly scream.

I stopped instantly. Brad was unable to halt his run, and he smashed into me. I was knocked forward, but I didn't fall.

"Why don't you look where you're going?!?" I scolded.

"Why don't you go where I'm looking?!?!" Brad shot right back.

Another scream suddenly pierced the dark night. It was an awful, terrorizing shriek.

"No! No! Stop!" I could hear the voice plead. *"No! Pleeeeeeaaaaassssssse!"*

And we knew who it was. The voice belonged to none other than Cully McGinty.

And we also knew that something *terrible* had happened.

"That way!" I shouted, pointing in the direction of Cully's screams. *"He's over there!"*

And we were off again, sailing through the inky darkness.

We could no longer hear anything from Cully, and I feared the worst.

Had the three dark ninjas attacked him? I thought. *Or maybe the white one?* I still didn't know enough about what was going on to figure anything out.

What a strange Halloween this was turning out to be.

We cut through a backyard and beneath a

clump of dark trees. There was no sign or sound from Cully.

I stopped running. "He has to be around here somewhere," I said, peering into the shadows. I could see dark shadows behind houses and garages. Tall, leafless trees cast long, wisping shadows across lawns.

"He has to be close," Sarah said, turning her head and searching the shadows.

And suddenly—

A noise. It was faint, but it sounded like . . .

"Wait a minute!" Sarah whispered excitedly. *"That's . . . that's . . . ."*

A deep growl suddenly came from the shadows behind one of the houses.

"That's Comet!" Sarah finished. *"I know it is! I'd know his growl anywhere!"*

We started walking in the direction of Comet's growling.

Now we could hear something else.

In the darkness, we could hear Cully McGinty whimpering. He sounded like he was scared to death!

"Cully!?!?" I called out. *"Where are you?"*

112

"Call him off!" Cully cried. "I'll give you your stupid mask back! Just . . . just call off the dog!"

We still couldn't see him, and we rushed in the direction of his voice.

"There he is!" Brad blurted out. "Over there! Against that shed!"

Brad was right. I could see Cully's dark silhouette pinned against the shed. In front of him, the threatening, dark shape of Comet loomed, poised and ready to attack.

"I told you!" Cully screamed. *"You can have your stupid mask back! Just get him away! Call him off!"*

"Comet!" Sarah commanded. "Sit!"

Comet stopped barking and did as Sarah ordered.

"Here!" Cully shouted, throwing the mask toward us. It landed on the grass at my feet, and I scooped it up.

Cully didn't say anything more. He got to his feet and bolted off into the darkness. Comet gave a few short growls as Cully's footsteps faded off.

"Good boy," Sarah said to her dog. She placed her witch hat back on her head and walked up to Comet. She patted his head, and the dog thumped his tail happily.

"I thought you gave him a time out for eating my candy," Brad said.

"Well, not for the entire night," Sarah replied.

I looked at the mask in my hands.

"Now what?" I asked. "Where are we supposed to take this thing?"

"I wonder if we could find the spooky white ninja again," Brad asked.

We all looked around. A few other kids in costumes were still out trick-or-treating, or on their way to the Halloween party at the school. I could hear some of them talking and laughing.

But that was it. There was no white ninja, no dark ninjas, nothing.

Maybe this is all just one big Halloween joke, I thought. *Maybe this is just someone's idea of playing a prank on us.*

But the more I thought about it, the more I realized that what had happened was no joke. The three of us had all seen the same things: the three dark ninjas, the white ninja, the mask in the sky.

114

There was something freaky going on, that was for sure.

But we had no idea what we were supposed to do. We didn't know where the sacred ground was, where the ninjas had vanished to.

Nothing.

And then Sarah found something in the grass that changed *everything*.

Sarah found the clue that the white ninja had promised.

The three of us, along with Comet, were walking across the darkened yard. We were silent, each of us wondering what to do or where to go.

Suddenly, Sarah stopped. She bent over and picked something up without speaking.

Brad and I stopped.

"What is it?" I asked.

"It's some sort of book," she replied, turning it over in her hands.

I drew closer and peered at the book in her hands.

"It was just laying in the grass?" Brad asked.

"Yeah," Sarah replied. "I almost stepped on it."

"Let's take it under the streetlight and see what it is," I said, and we walked to the street, stopping at the curb. Comet sat down in the grass.

The book was the size of a school textbook, only it appeared to be very old.

"The cover feels like it's made of leather," Sarah said.

She handed it to me, and I looked at the cover.

"There's no title or anything," I said, flipping the book over. There was nothing written on the back, either.

"Open it up," Brad said.

I was still carrying the Kabuki mask, and I tucked it beneath my arm and opened up the book to the first page.

"Look!" I gasped. "Look what it says!"

Sarah and Brad leaned closer, and all three of us read the words out loud.

"The Legend of the Mask of the Masters," we read slowly.

"The clue!" I exclaimed. *"This must be the clue*

that the white ninja told us he would send!"

"Wow!" Brad exclaimed. "This night just gets stranger and stranger."

I flipped through the book. The pages were old and yellowed, and the ink had run in some places. It was still readable, and I skimmed over a few paragraphs.

"This seems to be some sort of handbook," I said. "Kind of like an owner's manual?" Sarah asked.

"No, not really. I think it's more of a history book. Look." I pointed at a page. "This talks all about the legend of the mask. And back here—" I paused as I flipped to the back of the book. "—here it tells about how the mask was created and why."

I studied a page, then flipped to another. It was plain to see that the strange white ninja had been right, after all. The mask had been created for a warrior princess, but it had been stolen, just like that creepy white ninja said! It had surfaced several times over the past few hundred years, only to be sold or stolen again. Finally, it was purchased by a museum right here in Albany . . .

only to be stolen again years ago. No one has seen the mask since.

"Well, then that means that this is stolen property,"
Brad said. "It belongs to a museum."

"But that white ninja guy said that we have to return it to some 'sacred ground'" I replied. "I wonder where that is supposed to be."

I had spoken the words as I turned the page, still inspecting the strange manual.

"*There!*" Brad said, snapping out his arm and placing a finger on the page. "Right here! What's it say about 'sacred ground'?"

I began reading out loud.

"*Whoever finds the mask will be in danger of the curse of the dark ninja,*" I read slowly. "*The mask must be returned to sacred ground within four hours of touching the mask. If this is done, the great battle can begin, and the wicked dark ninjas will be defeated. The sacred ground is located —*"

I stopped reading, and my mouth hung open in disbelief.

"No," I said, shaking my head. "It can't be. It just *can't* be!"

Sarah and Brad drew closer to read what I was reading.

"Go where?" Brad asked. "Where is the sacred ground?" *"This book says that it is the old State Street Burial Grounds!"*

Brad's eyes got huge. "But that's ... that's —"

"I know," I said, interrupting him. "It's no longer a burial ground. But that's what it says here in the book."

The State Street Burial Ground was an old cemetery in the middle of Albany. In the 1840's, the cemetery was moved . . . bodies and everything . . . to the Albany Rural Cemetery. In its place, Washington Park was developed. It's a huge place, and there are a lot of events held there throughout the year. Every spring, a tulip festival is held, and it's a blast. Across the street from the park is Rockefeller College, which is where our mom works. We don't live far from it at all.

In fact, from where we stood, Washington Park was only a few blocks away!

"You mean . . . all we have to do is take the mask to the park?" Brad asked. "That'll be a cinch!"

"But what is this 'great battle' that it talks about?" Sarah asked.

I began reading again.

"The great battle between the good and evil ninjas will take place on the sacred ground. This battle will only begin when the mask is returned. After the battle, the mask will be returned to its final resting place."

"That's nuts!" Brad said. "This has to be some sort of joke!"

"Where in the park, exactly, does it say we have to take the mask?" Sarah asked.

I flipped through the pages.

"It doesn't," I replied.

"Maybe we have to bury it in the ground or something," Brad mused. "Or do some kind of special dance around it."

"Don't be a kook," I said.

"Well, whatever we do, we'd better get started," Sarah said. "We don't have much time left."

Sarah was right. We had better get a move on and get to the park . . . or the 'sacred ground', as the white ninja had described it.

I gave the book to Sarah to carry, and we set out for Washington Park. Soon, the houses gave way to bigger buildings. We crossed Washington Avenue, and I could see the lights of the park.

"Almost there," I said.

I spoke way too soon.

Suddenly, Sarah stopped. She pointed.

"*Look!*" she exclaimed.

I turned to see where she was pointing, and I realized that we might not make it to Washington Park, after all.

Standing beneath a tree, hiding in the murky shadows, were three figures.

Ninjas.

And suddenly, without warning, they began spinning and flipping, twisting and turning. When we had spotted them before, they had pretty much left us alone.

But now, it was different.

Now, they were coming right for us!

I felt like we were trapped in some kind of crazy movie. The three ninjas kicked and jabbed as they came toward us, spinning and whirling.

"*Run!*" I shouted, and the three of us took off in different directions. Comet followed on Sarah's heels.

"Hang onto the mask, Mike!" Sarah shouted. "Try and get into the park with it!"

We were off.

I sprinted down the street and managed a glance over my shoulder. The three ninjas had stopped their pursuit and were now in the middle of the street, frozen, ready for action.

Man, was I glad that they weren't chasing us anymore. There was no way I wanted to get into a fight with one of those guys . . . *let alone all three!*

I didn't waste any time in running across the street. Farther up the road, I saw Brad and Sarah do the same thing.

If I can make it to the park, I can meet up with them, I thought.

I sped around parked cars and ducked behind a tree to catch my breath. Slowly, I peered around the huge trunk to catch a glimpse of the ninjas.

They were gone!

But I was sure they'd be back. I figured that they would do anything to stop me before I reached the sacred ground.

I turned and started up the street. It was still early, and several cars passed by. A few college students walked by me, and I heard them laugh after I had passed. They were probably laughing at my costume. I had forgotten that I was still dressed as a vampire.

Soon, the park entrance was in view, and I knew that I could be inside in seconds.

I was going to make it.

What I needed to do with the mask once I was in the park . . . well, I hadn't a clue. I guess I'd find out soon enough.

I *hoped* I would, anyway. I certainly didn't want some ninja curse upon me for the rest of my life.

I turned to walk into the park, but it was obvious I wasn't going to get very far.

Without warning, a large, dark figure sprang from the bushes. He lunged for me, and there was nothing I could do.

I was sent flying, and the mask flew out from beneath my arm.

I jumped up instantly, only to be knocked to the ground again. I rolled away and stood up quickly, ready to defend myself.

"Gotcha this time!" I heard a gruff voice say. I spun around and saw Cully McGinty, his hands doubled into fists, coming toward me.

"Leave me alone!" I demanded.

"You don't have that silly witch or that goofy ghost to help you now," he snapped. "Or that stupid dog."

Now he was right up to my face.

"I'm warning you," I said as bravely as I could. Actually, I was pretty scared, but I didn't want Cully to know it.

"I'm taking that mask," he stated flatly. "I bet it's worth some money."

Suddenly he lunged for the mask in the grass . . . but I was quicker.

Before he reached it, I had already sprung, diving to the grass and scooping the mask up. I held it to my chest as I rolled away, and Cully hit the ground a second too late. He landed with a thud, but I was already several yards away and getting to my feet.

Cully was more than just *mad*. He was *livid*.

"You've done it now, shrimp!" he screamed angrily, scrambling to his feet. "You just wait 'till I get my hands on you! You just wait 'till—"

He stopped speaking, and I turned around as I fled.

Then I stopped.

Cully was surrounded by the three ninjas!

"What the—" I heard Cully say. The three ninjas were circled around him, standing in fighting positions.

And then Cully relaxed. A grin came to his face. "Oh, I get it," he sneered. "Halloween. You guys are in costume. Well, you look ridiculous. Where did you get your costume, from your sister's bedroom?"

From the reaction of the three dark ninjas, it was probably the worst thing that Cully could have said.

Maybe they were mad because he had insulted them. For whatever reason, Cully was suddenly sent sailing through the air . . . and I mean *sailing!*

He spun over my head and landed on the ground in a heaping thud. It happened so fast that Cully couldn't do a thing. The ninjas had flung Cully up into the air like he was some kind of toy!

For a moment, I though that he might be hurt. He remained on the ground, motionless.

The three dark ninjas remained where they were, ready for battle.

Slowly, Cully raised his head. He turned and looked back at the three shadowy figures.

In the next instant he was up and off, running like a mad jackrabbit, screaming his head off! It was kind of funny, actually. I was glad that he wasn't hurt, but I was also glad that he got what was coming to him.

But now I had *another* problem.

Actually, three problems, and they were standing in front of the park entrance. There was no way I could get around them.

Suddenly, I heard a shout from inside the park! Something moved, and I caught a glimpse of Brad as he appeared from the shadows. In the next instant, Sarah was by his side, followed by Comet.

My eyes flashed from the three ninjas to my two friends. Brad and Sarah were far enough away from the ninjas to be out of danger, but I was only a few feet from the dark figures.

I wasn't sure what to do. I knew that, somehow, I had to get into the park.

But there was no way I would be able to fight my way past the three ninjas!

And then, without warning, the three ninjas attacked. So far, I had been lucky. Up until now, the three ninjas hadn't really posed much of a problem, and I hadn't needed to defend myself.

Now, however, it was a different story. The three ninjas knew that I was near the sacred ground. They knew what I was doing, and where I was going. They knew what my intentions were.

And now, they were going to stop me.

Whirling and spinning, legs and arms a blur, the three ninjas attacked, coming straight at me.

I tried to run . . . but it was already far too late. I was flung back and into the air, landing on my back in the soft grass. I didn't even know what had happened!

But I knew this much: the three ninjas weren't through with me.

And as I lay on the ground clutching the ancient mask, the three hooded figures came at me once again for a final, devastating attack.

There was nothing I, Brad, or Sarah could do. It was over. I had failed to get the mask to the sacred ground, and the three ninjas would soon have the mask in their possession.

I closed my eyes, waiting for the brutal assault.

The three ninjas leapt into the air, and I knew that, in seconds, I would be pulverized.

But—

The blows never came!

From the park, I heard Sarah and Brad gasp. There were several heavy thuds, and I opened my eyes just in time to see the three ninjas tumble to the ground.

"Mike! Behind you!" Sarah shouted.

I was still on the ground clutching the mask to my chest, and I turned to see the *white* ninja towering above me! He was standing in a fighting stance, ready for battle. Man . . . was I glad to see him!

"Now!" he thundered. "You must go! Get to the sacred ground!"

That was all I needed to hear. I jumped up, spun, and turned to run.

BAM!

In the next instant, I was on the ground again! One of the ninjas had attacked!

The white ninja sprang to my defense, and suddenly all four ninjas were locked in battle.

It was the opportunity I needed.

I leapt to my feet, determined to make it through the park entrance.

"*Hurry, Mike!*" Brad shouted. "*You can make it!*"

I took huge steps, bounding across the grass and onto a slab of pavement. I didn't look back, didn't turn my head or anything. I focused only on making it into the park.

And then:

I made it! I was through! I was inside Washington Park!

I didn't slow down until I reached Sarah and

Brad. They were standing in the shadows beneath a tree.

"You did it!" Sarah exclaimed as I came to a stop next to her. I was gasping for breath, and I could feel my heart pounding in my chest.

The three of us turned to see the strange sight near the entrance of the park. The ninjas were still engaged in battle, but suddenly, as we watched, the white ninja simply vanished! He was gone!

The three dark ninjas looked around in confusion. Their heads spun around, looking to see where their opponent had gone.

"Where did he go?" Brad asked.

I shook my head. " Don't ask me. You saw the same thing I did," I replied.

And then: the three ninjas spun off into the night. Again, they didn't just walk or run. The whirled and twirled and spun about, doing flips and hand-springs, their arms and legs flying. In two seconds, they had vanished into the dark night.

"Man, am I glad that's over with," I said. "I thought I was going to be karate-chopped into a billion pieces!"

I breathed a sigh of relief, not knowing that the *real* trouble was about to begin.

And it all started when Comet began to growl.

When Comet started growling, we all turned to see what had caused him to become alarmed.

And let me say this: we weren't prepared for what we were seeing.

All around us, Washington Park was changing . . . right before our eyes! Trees were vanishing, and buildings were appearing in their place! It was the most bizarre thing I had ever seen. Soon, the entire landscape had changed, and the park was now unrecognizable. It looked nothing like Washington Park, and more like . . . *An ancient burial ground!*

"How can this be?" I asked quietly.

Sarah only shook her head, and we stood in silence, staring.

There were several buildings around us that looked to be made of stone. I thought that they might be tombs of some sort.

But the scariest thing of all was the fact that we could no longer see any other buildings. At least not the normal buildings that you should be able to see from Washington Park. The entrance to the park had vanished, and so had the buildings along the streets. It didn't even look anything like Albany anymore!

But then another thing began to appear. A ghostly white image began to materialize before us, becoming brighter and brighter. At first it seemed like a haze, but, after a few seconds, I recognized what it was.

The white ninja!

Brad spoke up instantly.

"Hey . . . ummm, Mr. Ninja-Dude," he stammered. "We brought the mask here. My brother has it. Can we go home now?"

We waited for a reply, but we didn't get the

answer that I wanted to hear.

"Yes, you have brought the Mask of the Masters to the sacred ground. It has been many years since the mask has been here. However, it will be very difficult for you to simply leave."

"Wait a minute!" I exclaimed angrily. "We did what you asked! You said that I had to bring the mask to the sacred ground, or else live with the curse of the dark ninja!" The more I spoke, the angrier I became. "We don't even know what's going on! I found the mask and we got chased around by three dark ninjas. Then, you appeared and told us about coming here. We did everything you asked!"

The white ninja nodded. "That is true," he replied. "You have. But there are some things that must remain unexplained to you. There are some things you cannot know, for your own safety."

That didn't make much sense to me, and I was still angry. The white ninja continued speaking.

"There are some things that you would not understand, even if I explained them to you. Just know this: know that you have helped a great deal by returning the mask to this sacred ground. Now, the battle can begin. Now, we can finally defeat our enemies."

Again, I was more confused than anything.

"But who are your enemies?" Brad asked.

"The dark ninjas of the night," the white ninja replied. "They are our enemies. They want the Mask of the Masters, and they will fight to the end."

I looked at the mask in my hands. It sure had caused lot of trouble.

"But what did you mean when you said that it would be difficult for us to leave?" Sarah asked.

The white ninja paused.

"The battle will begin when the Mask of the Masters is laid to rest in the Master's Tomb." He turned and pointed to a large, brick building not far away. "When it is finally laid to rest, the dark ninjas will return for one final attempt to steal it. It is then that we must defeat them once and for all."

"But . . . can't we just put the mask in the tomb and leave?" I asked. " I mean . . . it's already getting late. Our parents will ground us until the next century if we don't get home soon."

"Oh, I believe that you will make it home," the white ninja replied. "It is just going to be difficult. Here is what you will need to do."

And when he explained what was about to happen, I freaked. So did Brad and Sarah.

As if things weren't strange already, what was about to happen was simply *unbelievable*.

31

We would have to somehow get out of the sacred burial ground — Washington Park — while *hundreds* of ninja warriors were engaged in battle!

"When the battle begins, it will take all of our strength to fight off the forces of the dark ninjas. I will not be able to help you. You can escape, but it will be difficult."

"But . . . but what if we don't escape?" Sarah asked.

"Yeah," Brad chimed in. "I have homework that I have to do."

The white ninja didn't answer.

"Come. I will show you where to place the mask."

I held it out. "Here," I offered. "Why don't you do it?"

The ninja shook his head. "It must be placed in the tomb by the person who found it," he said. "That is the only way."

Rats. I thought that if he could place the mask in the tomb for me, then we could get a head start out of this place — before the battle had started.

"Come," the ninja said. He turned and began to walk away.

I looked at Sarah and Brad, and they looked at me.

"You guys stay here," I said. "I'll go put this in the tomb, and I'll be right back."

Sarah and Brad nodded, and I started out after the white ninja.

I looked around, looking for any sign of Washington Park.

Nothing. It was as if the park no longer existed. In its place was a strange, dark land. I had no idea where I was . . . but I was sure that it wasn't Albany!

The white ninja led me to a tomb with a large door. He stood back, and gestured for me to move forward.

"You must be the one who opens the door," he said.

Man, when I found this mask, I never realized everything I would be going through! If I knew then what I know now, I would have never touched the thing!

I stepped up to the door. There was some kind of writing on it, but it was hard to see in the dark. I did, however, see a large handle, and I reached out and grasped it. I tried pulling, but the door wouldn't budge.

Then I pushed it.

Instantly the giant door began to swing open, and a strange, green light glowed from inside. It was really eerie looking, and I turned around to see if Brad and Sarah were watching. I saw them standing alone, watching me.

The white ninja spoke. "Listen carefully. Go inside and place the mask on the table in the middle."

I pushed the door open farther, and, sure

enough, there was a table in the middle of the tomb. It was all glass and there was a single empty cloth on the top of it. I was sure that it was the place I would need to set the mask.

I entered the tomb and walked to the middle of the small room. All along the walls, ancient swords and knives hung. It was like being in a museum.

I gently placed the mask on the table. It seemed so easy, such a simple thing to do. I wondered what the big deal was all about.

Regardless, I wanted to get out of there. I wanted to return to Sarah and Brad.

And I wanted to go home.

I exited the tomb and was about to pull the door closed when I stopped — and froze in horror.

32.

Ninjas, both black and white, were everywhere. As far as I could see. There were *hundreds* of them.

Thousands of them.

And Brad and Sarah where nowhere in sight, lost in the sea of ninjas.

The white ninja that had led me to the tomb was standing near.

"The only way from this world back to your world will be through the ancient white wall," he said. "You must find the wall, and leap through it. It is the only way. Go now!"

Instantly, the battle began, and I knew that I was in big trouble. All around me, legs were spinning, arms were whirling, and ninjas were leaping and flipping into the air! The noise was deafening.

In the next moment, I was sent flying. Now I could see what the white ninja had meant: it was going to be difficult to get out of here without getting hurt. Even though I wasn't actually involved in the battle, there were so many fighting ninjas that it would be nearly impossible to keep from being dragged into the melee!

I scrambled to my feet and immediately had to duck to keep from being kicked in the head by a flying leg. Getting out of here . . . however we would do it . . . was going to be more than tricky.

"Mike!" I heard Sarah shout. I spun in the direction of her voice, but I couldn't see her.

"Mike!" I heard her shout again.

This time, I caught a quick glimpse of her in the distance. She had lost her witch hat. Brad was next to her, and both of them were trying hard to keep away from all of the warring ninjas.

I tried to run toward them, but again I was

knocked to the ground. It hurt that time, and I realized that we were in serious danger.

I figured the best way to make it to Sarah and Brad would be to crawl on my hands and knees. If I stayed low, maybe I could keep out of the way.

Problem was, I was surrounded by fighting ninjas. They were everywhere, and even as I crawled I was being knocked around and bumped all over the place. The ninjas really weren't paying any attention to me, but I sure was trying to stay out of their way.

On and on I crawled, weaving in and around the fighters. I hoped I was going in the direction of Sarah and Brad. With everything going on, I really couldn't tell.

Then: I got lucky. I caught a glimpse of Brad's white sheet. Actually, I was surprised that I even recognized him, since he looked so much like one of the fighting white ninjas!

"Brad!" I shouted.

He turned and saw me, then he, too, fell to his hands and knees. Soon, the three of us were together again. Comet was there, too, but he wasn't the brave Comet that he usually was. Now he seemed frightened, and his tail was tucked between his legs.

"How do we get out of here?!?!" Sarah shouted.

"I don't know!" I replied. "I can't see anything!"

"Let's try heading back to where the entrance to the park should be!" Brad screamed.

Of course, the entrance to the park was no longer visible, but it was the only chance we had. One thing was for sure: we had to take cover from the fighting ninjas. We were in the middle of their battle, and at any moment we could become victims of their powerful kicking and jabbing.

"This way!" I shouted, instantly taking the lead. We scrambled as fast as we could on our hands and knees, heading in the direction of where I thought the park entrance would be. All around us the battle raged.

And suddenly . . . another stroke of luck! Up ahead, through the dozens of spinning ninjas, I could see a large, white square!

The way out! If we could make it to the wall, we would be safe.

"There it is!" I shouted. "Up ahead!"

Suddenly, Comet sprang. He charged ahead, slinking in and around the ninjas.

When he reached the white wall, he didn't even hesitate. He plunged headfirst into the white void . . . *and vanished!*

"That's it!" Sarah cried. *"That's the way out!"*

We crawled along the ground as fast as we could. I received several sharp kicks from the ninjas around us, but fortunately, they weren't serious.

"Almost there!" I shouted. "We're going to make it!"

But, as fate would have it, it wasn't quite that simple.

I reached the white wall first, then Sarah.

Brad was nowhere to be found.

"Brad!" I screamed. I peered through the mob of fighting ninjas, but I didn't see any sign of him.

"Where did he go?!?!" Sarah shouted. "He was right next to me!"

Suddenly, Sarah and I had to duck out of the way of a fierce, karate-style kick administered by one of the dark ninjas. His foot missed my head by inches!

That was too close for comfort. If we didn't go through the white wall soon, there was no telling what might happen.

"Sarah!" I ordered. *"Go through the wall! I'll look for Brad!"*

"No way!" she replied over the noise of a thousand ninjas. *"I'll help find him!"*

"No! You'll get hurt!"

"I will not!"

There was no point in arguing with her, but it was far too dangerous for Sarah . . . no matter how tough she might be.

Without wasting another second, I grabbed her by the shoulders. With every muscle I had I pushed her through the wall. She cried out in surprise, only for an instant, and then she was gone.

Sarah was safe. She was going to be really mad at me when I came through the white wall, but at least she was safe.

I turned my attention back to the swarming mob of ninjas, straining to see through the crowd.

Suddenly, I saw Brad! He was standing up . . . and a dark ninja was right in front of him!

"Run, Brad, run!" I screamed.

He turned and fled—and not a moment too soon! The dark ninja had already leapt into the air and delivered a powerful jab with his arm . . . right where Brad had been standing!

Brad had disappeared once again, but I was sure that he'd dropped down on his hands and knees.

I hoped he had, anyway.

Tense seconds ticked by. Thankfully, I was able to stay back from the battling warriors.

And then:

Brad!

He popped to his feet as he dodged out of the way of two ninjas locked in hand-to-hand combat.

"Hurry!" I shouted. "Before you get dragged into the fight!"

Brad spun around and was able to evade several more clashing ninjas. Then he was suddenly struck by accident . . . and he fell, landing right at my feet!

"Get up!" I shouted. I'd see if he was okay later. My main concern was to get through that white wall and get back to Albany.

I helped Brad up. He seemed to be alright, just a bit dazed.

There was no more time to lose. Together, we leapt into and through the white wall.

And suddenly . . . .

We were in Albany!

But, then again, maybe we had never left.

We came through the white wall with such force that we tumbled right into Sarah. All three of us fell to the ground in a heap, and Comet joined in by licking my face. I pushed him away and stood up.

"Wow!" I exclaimed. "I can't believe that just happened!"

Looking around, the night was like any other night in October. Several people were walking about, and I saw a couple of them still in their Halloween costumes. Cars passed by on the street.

And behind me—

Washington Park!

It looked just like it always did. There was no white wall, no fighting ninja warriors. No noise.

Suddenly, there was a sharp jab on my shoulder. Not real hard, but hard enough. I turned to see Sarah, holding her fist up. She looked angry.

"That was for pushing me through that white wall," she snapped.

"I didn't want you to get hurt," I said. "I wanted to make sure that you made it out okay."

Brad scrambled to his feet. "I'm glad you guys saw the same things I did," he said. "No one is going to believe any of this!"

"They'll have to!" I exclaimed. "We can show them the book!"

An expression of sorrow fell over Sarah's face.

"I . . . I . . . dropped it," she said finally. "When my hat fell off I tried to catch it . . . and I lost both the hat and the book."

That was a bummer. The book would have proven to everyone what had happened.

"We've got to get home," I said. "It's getting pretty late."

The three of us crossed the street and headed for our block. We talked the entire time, recalling the different things that had happened that evening.

And we wondered a lot of different things. Would we ever see a white ninja again? Or a dark ninja? Everything had happened so fast, and we still had so many questions. Is there some kind of weird world where the ninjas live? If so, had anyone else discovered it?

I guess it was like the white ninja had said. Some things we just aren't meant to understand.

But maybe the ninjas will return, I thought. *Maybe they will come back. What if the mask is stolen again?*

No. The white ninja said that this would be the final battle.

I sure hoped that the white ninjas won. The thought of those dark ninjas running through our neighborhood gave me the creeps.

We said good-bye to Sarah, and I told her that we would see her in the morning. The three of us were going to go back to Washington Park to see if there was any sign at all from the great battle we had witnessed.

We had just crossed the street and were almost to the porch of our house when we realized our troubles weren't over.

Standing in the shadows of the bushes, was a figure.

Not just *any* figure.

A dark ninja.

I screamed and leapt back. Brad let out a shriek
and spun.

The ninja attacked. He leapt out from the
bushes, his arms flailing madly, spinning like fan
blades.

"Hi-yaa! Ka-CHAA!" the ninja screeched.

Wait a minute, I thought. *That voice sounds
familiar!*

"Ka-YAAA! CHAA!" the dark ninja said, and
I let out a sigh of relief. That was no dark ninja!
That was *Dad!*

"Hahahaha!" he said in his normal voice.

"Gotcha, didn't I?"

"You didn't scare me," I said.

"Me neither," Brad chimed in, walking back up to the porch.

Okay, maybe Dad scared us a little.

"And you said you didn't like my ninja warrior costume," Dad said proudly. "I fooled you guys!"

"Yeah, well wait until we tell you about what happened to us!" Brad said.

We went inside and my brother and I explained everything that happened. Mom and Dad listened, but I knew they didn't believe us.

But that very night, something strange happened that, even to this day, no one in Albany can explain.

But Sarah, Brad and I can.

And it started when I received a frantic phone call from Sarah. It was early Saturday morning, and no one else was even up yet, including myself. I was the first to reach the phone.

"Turn on your radio, quick!" she said.

"Huh?" I replied sleepily. It was pretty early in the morning.

"Turn on your radio! You're not going to believe what happened during the night!"

I flew back into my bedroom and flipped on my radio. The news was on, and I listened.

I couldn't believe what I was hearing!

They were talking about an ancient artifact that had been missing from the New York State Museum for years . . . *an artifact that had mysteriously re-appeared in the museum overnight!*

There had been no break-in, and nothing was stolen. The people at the museum were at a loss to explain who returned the artifact, or how.

Or *why.*

They did, however, say what the artifact was:

An ancient Japanese Kabuki mask!

Talk about being freaked out!

I ran to Brad's room, woke him up, and told him about it. At first, he didn't believe me, but I think he finally realized how serious I was.

"We've got to go see it!" he exclaimed. "I wonder if it's the same mask that you found! Maybe that's what the book meant when it talked about it being returned to its final place of rest."

"But how would it get in the museum?" I asked.

"Hey . . . after last night, I'll believe anything," Brad replied, nodding his head.

Later that day, Brad, Sarah and I rode our bikes over to the museum. The New York State Museum is really cool. There are a lot of exhibits, and we spent a lot more time looking around than we'd actually intended.

We had become separated while we were looking around, when I suddenly heard Sarah gasp from up ahead.

"*Brad! Mike! Come and look!*" she said excitedly. She was standing by a dimly-lit glass jewel case. I rushed up to her, and Brad came from around a corner.

Inside the jewel case, secured by locks, was the mask.

Not *a* mask.

The mask.

The same Japanese Kabuki mask that I had found! I was sure of it.

"That's really wild," I said.

Sarah shook her head.

That was the weirdest Halloween I've ever had," she said.

"For us too," I replied.

On Monday, we returned to school and explained what happened to us—but no one believed a single word!

Even though all three of us tried to explain about the mask and the ninjas and the great battle, not one single person believed us! We didn't even have the book to show them!

I even called the museum that evening and explained to them. They were polite, but the guy laughed and told me to stop kidding around. *Besides,* he had said, *the police dusted it for fingerprints. There were none on the mask.*

But just when I thought things couldn't get any weirder . . . the telephone rang.

Dad answered the phone and called for me.

"Some kid named Jake," he said, handing me the receiver.

Jake? I thought. *I don't know anyone by the name of Jake. I'll bet he's got the wrong number.*

"Hello?" I said.

"Mike?" a voice on the line said.

"Yeah?" I replied. I didn't recognize the voice.

"This is Jake Sherwood. I'm in another class at school. You don't know me."

Jake explained that he'd heard about our story, about the mask and the ninjas.

"Everybody's talking about it," he said.

"Yeah, everyone's *laughing* about it," I said dryly. "No one believes a single word we said. But it's true. Every single bit of it."

"I believe it," Jake said. "I *really* do."

I paused.

"You . . . you do?" I asked.

"Yep," he said. "My family and I just moved here from Texas, and after what happened to me, I'd believe just about anything."

"What?" I asked him. "What happened to you in Texas?"

"If I tell you, I'll bet you won't believe it, even after the strange things that happened to you."

Now, I was *really* curious.

"Tell me," I urged.

"I'll tell you," he said, "but you have to promise not to tell anyone at school. People will think I'm crazy."

"Promise," I said.

And Jake began his story, which, I soon found out, was every bit as freaky as he said . . . .

172

next in the

AMERICAN CHILLERS

series:

#5:Terrible Tractors of Texas

turn the page to read a few spine-chilling chapters . . . if you dare!

1

"*Jake! It's five-thirty! Get a move on!*"

I groaned. Dad was yelling from outside, and he knew I wasn't out of bed yet. I'm usually up by five in the morning to begin my chores around the farm. Today, however, I was really tired, and I'd fallen back to sleep.

I groaned again, and climbed out of bed.

Might as well get started, I thought.

The roosters were already crowing, and I could hear the hens clucking near the barn. Our family has a small ranch about a hundred miles from Dallas, Texas. We have chickens, horses, hogs, cows . . . the usual farm animals. I wouldn't trade it for the world, but sometimes, the work can be pretty boring.

175

Today, however, would be different. My best friend, John Culver, was coming. He used to be my neighbor when we lived in Houston, but we moved away to the farm a couple of years ago. I don't get to see him much anymore.

But today he would be coming to spend the whole *week* with us! John is eleven, the same age as me. We have always got along great, and we like a lot of the same things.

And it was July. The middle of summer vacation. School wouldn't be starting for another two months!

Not that I don't like school, because I do. It's just that summer in Texas is so much *fun*.

With John visiting, the coming week was going to be nothing but fun with a capital 'F'.

At least, that's what I thought when I got up that morning. I thought that we'd spend the days fishing and swimming and biking.

That wasn't what would happen. Oh, we would have fun for a little while.

But by tonight, everything would change—and our fun would be over.

Our fun would be over . . . and the terror would begin.

2

I ate a quick bowl of corn flakes before heading outside. The sun was already coming up, and the eastern sky was all pink and yellow. If you ever come to Texas, don't miss the sunrises. We have some of the coolest sunrises in the world. The sunsets are beautiful, too.

It took me a couple of hours to take care of the animals. We have hired hands that help out, but it's always been my job to look after the livestock. It's hard work, and I'm not complaining.

It's just that I *really* wanted to get everything done before John got here. That way we would have all day to hang out. We could go down to the creek and fish, catch turtles and frogs . . . heck, we would have a *blast*.

I went into the barn to find more food for the geese. We have seven geese on the farm and when they don't get fed on time, they get really cranky. When they saw me coming this morning, they started honking and making all kinds of noise.

In the barn, we have several big pieces of farm equipment, including some really cool tractors. They're awesome! Dad used to take me for rides when I was little, but now I can operate them all by myself. One of the tractors—a big red one—is one that I drive a lot. It's my favorite.

There is some other heavy machinery we have, too. Dad bought a bulldozer and a small crane at an auction, but they're too big to put in the barn. When they're not being used, we keep them out back near the corral.

"Jake!" I heard Dad call out. I turned and walked out of the barn.

Dad was standing by a big green diesel storage tank. Most of the tractors and farm equipment run on diesel.

"Yeah?" I replied, squinting in the morning sun.

"I'm going into Dallas today. I'll need you to fill up all of the equipment for the workers. I want to use the new fuel in everything to see how it works."

Shoot, I thought. Fueling up all of the equipment would take another hour. And Dad bought this new experimental gas that is supposed to make the equipment run longer.

I had my doubts. Fuel is fuel. It wasn't going to make any difference.

I was wrong.

Really wrong.

The gas . . . the new experimental fuel that Dad wanted to try out in all the farm equipment . . . would do more than simply make the equipment run longer.

A *lot* more.

And when I fueled up all of the tractors and dozers and equipment with that gas, I had no way of knowing the trouble we were in for.

"Okay," I answered, and I turned and walked back into the barn.

Gas up everything?!?! I thought. *There is no way I'll finish before John gets here!*

By now, the geese were really making an awful lot of racket. They were hungry.

I had just walked out the front of the barn when I spotted something that made me freeze in my tracks. I didn't move, for I knew better.

And if you saw what I saw, you'd do the exact

same thing.

Right next to my foot, only inches away, was a rattlesnake.

A *big* one.

And he was coiled up, preparing to strike!

3

I didn't move a single muscle. That's the only thing you can do when you're confronted with a rattlesnake. I wear thick leather boots when I work, but that doesn't mean that a rattlesnake can't bite through them.

And if this one did, I'd be in *serious* trouble.

So, I froze like an ice cube.

The snake remained poised, ready to attack and sink its razor-sharp fangs into my leg.

And then:

Giggling. I heard giggling coming from the side of the barn!

I still hadn't moved an inch, but now I slowly

turned my head to see who was laughing.

"Haha! Gotcha!" a voice exclaimed.

John!

I relaxed, and took a step back from the snake. Obviously it was fake, but it sure was a *good* fake! It really looked like an actual, coiled rattler!

"Isn't that cool?" John said.

"That's awesome!" I replied.

"It's yours. I bought it at a store for you. I have one, too, and I fool *everybody* with it!"

"For me?!?!" I exclaimed. "Gosh . . . thanks!"

I picked up the fake snake and looked at him.

"When did you get here?" I asked.

"Just a few minutes ago. Our car is in the driveway on the other side of your house. My mom and dad are inside, talking to your mom and dad."

"Help me finish up, and we'll head down to the creek," I said. "I'm almost done. We just have to gas up the equipment."

"Cool!"

I put the coiled snake on a fencepost, and we got to work. With John's help, it didn't take long to finish up with the livestock.

Then it was time to fuel up the equipment. I drove the tractors out of the barn and up to the fueling tank. That didn't take too long, either. After filling each tractor, I drove them back into the barn.

However, since I'm not allowed to drive the heavy equipment out back, we'd have to take the gas to the machinery. I wish I could, but Dad says not for a few more years.

John and I filled up a couple of five-gallon cans and carried them back to the big dozers and cranes. With both of us working at it, we'd be finished in no time at all.

"This gas smells funny," John said as we filled up the last piece of equipment. "It smells like rotten bananas."

"It's some kind of experimental gas that Dad wants to try out. He says it's supposed to be better than regular gas."

"It stinks," he said, holding his nose.

Just then, I heard shouting. A *girl* shouting. And she wasn't very far away.

I turned, puzzled by the noise. I don't have any brothers or sisters.

"That's the bad news," John said dryly. "My little sister is going to stay here all week, too."

Oh no! Janey is a whiney little brat!

"You're kidding?!?!" I said.

John shook his head. "I wish I was," he replied. "But Mom asked her if she wanted to stay, and she said yes. She's never been to a farm before. Your parents said that it was okay, too. So . . . we're stuck with her."

What a drag. Janey is a pest. She'd want to tag along with us everywhere we go!

Then I had an idea.

"Let's hide from her!" I hissed. "Maybe we can sneak off down to the creek without her!"

"Good thinking!" John agreed.

I finished filling up the dozer and wiped my hands on a rag. I could hear Janey calling out, trying to find us.

However, we were behind the barn and she was in front. She couldn't see us!

John peered around the corner.

"Can you see her?" I asked.

"She just went into the barn," John replied.

"Cool! Let's make a run for it! She'll never find us!"

We darted around a crane and ran along the corral . . . but we didn't get very far.

Suddenly, Janey began screaming. Not a fake, girly scream . . . *but a scream of all-out terror!*

4

Janey's screams were awful. Whatever was going on was *serious*.

John and I both stopped, kicking up a cloud of dust. We immediately spun and began running around to the front of the barn.

"She's never screamed like that before!" John huffed as we raced to help.

"She sounds like she's really hurt!" I said.

We darted around the corner of the barn and raced inside. Janey's screams of terror continued.

"Over there!" I cried. *"She's over there! On the other side of the tractors!"*

I knew that something had to be horribly, horribly

wrong.

We sprinted past the equipment to find Janey flat against the back of the barn! She was scared stiff, and her eyes were bugging out of her head!

And right in front of her, two feet away, was the reason for her fear.

A goose.

A plain old, ordinary goose.

It honked a couple of times, pecked the ground, then honked some more.

"What's wrong?!?!" I shouted.

Janey was still shrieking like crazy, and I placed my hands over my ears.

"The giant ducky is attacking me!!" Janey screeched. She had backed up against the wall, and she couldn't go any farther.

"For crying out loud," I said. "It's not a giant ducky! It's just a silly goose. He won't hurt you!"

"He attacked me!" Janey repeated. She was crying now, and she wouldn't budge one inch from the wall. "He's trying to eat me!"

"He didn't attack you," I said. "He just thinks that you have food for him. He's not going to eat you."

"Remember . . . she's never been to a farm before," John whispered *"Just be glad she didn't see a goat."*

I smiled, and walked up to the goose.

"Go on," I said, waving my hand at the bird. "Git! Get outside!"

The goose scooted beneath a tractor, clucking and honking.

"See?" John said. "It was only a goose. He's not going to hurt you."

"He had big teeth and he tried to bite me!"

I rolled my eyes.

"Geese don't have teeth," I insisted. "Come on, John."

As soon as John and I turned to leave, Janey unglued herself from the wall and began to follow.

"Huh-uh," John said, shaking his head. "He stopped to face her. "You're not coming."

"Mom says I can."

"I say you can't."

"I'll tell Daddy."

"Daddy doesn't like you. He's going to swap you for a set of golf clubs."

"Is not!"

"Is too!"

"Is not!"

"Is too!"

This was going nowhere, fast.

"Enough!" I said loudly. "Janey . . . you can come

with us . . . *if* you promise to leave us alone."

"I promise!" she said, bobbing her head.

"Come on, John," I said. The three of us walked past the parked tractors and out the door.

Suddenly, I stopped.

Something was wrong. There was something odd about one of the tractors.

"What?" John asked. "What's the matter?"

"I . . . I'm not sure," I replied.

My eyes scanned a few of the machines. There were several tractors and an old push lawn mower parked in a cluster, right where I'd left them. One of the tractors—the red one that I drive a lot—was parked near the door.

"This tractor," I said curiously. "It's . . . it's . . . ."

I paused. John and Janey were silent, waiting for me to finish.

"Oh my gosh!" I suddenly exclaimed. I leapt back, pulling John and Janey with me. *"This tractor! Look at it! It's it's alive! It's coming to life! We have to get out of here!"*

5

Janey screamed.

John screamed.

I screamed, too. As loud as I could.

The three of us whirled and started to run.

"It's coming!" I shouted. *"It's right behind us!"*

Janey was in front of us and she ran like lightning, screaming her head off.

I slowed, and I grabbed John's arm. He slowed, too.

"Okay, okay," I laughed. "That's good enough."

John suddenly realized that I had only been playing a prank on Janey.

"It worked!" he exclaimed. "Man . . . you even had *me* going!"

"I owed you one for scaring me with the snake," I smirked.

"Well, you sure got me back. Janey, too!"

Janey had never looked back. She ran across the driveway, over the yard, and disappeared into the house, screaming all the way.

"That was kind of a mean trick," John said. Then he flashed a crooked grin. "I wish I'd thought of it!"

We gave each other a high-five.

"Now," I said, "we can go to the creek without being bugged by your little sister."

We set out across the field. The creek isn't far away, and it only took a few minutes to reach it.

Just like I'd planned, we spent the day catching turtles and frogs and lizards. I even caught a small fish with my bare hands!

After a few hours, we hiked back to the farm. Some of the workers were in the field, and a couple of them were tending to the horses in the corral.

"This is going to be a great week," John said. "I'm glad you invited me."

"No problem," I said, "as long as you don't mind helping with the morning chores."

"Are you kidding? This is going to be the best week of the summer! I love it here!"

And then I had an idea.

"Hey . . . I'll take you for a ride on one of the tractors. Dad doesn't let me drive the real big ones behind the barn, but we can take one of the smaller ones from inside."

"Yeah!" John replied. "I've never ridden on a tractor before. My dad has an old riding mower, but that's pretty boring."

"These tractors are cool," I said. "They're really powerful."

By this time, I'd completely forgotten about the experimental gas. After we'd fueled up the farm equipment, I never even gave it another thought.

Until we walked into the barn. That's when things got really freaky.

The day was hot, but a sudden cold chill swept through me.

John stopped in his tracks and gasped.

And we both knew that what we were seeing was no joke.

The red tractor . . . the one I drive most of the time . . . was moving . . . *all by itself!*

Not only was it moving by itself—*it was coming right at us!*

ABOUT THE AUTHOR

Johnathan Rand is the author of more than 50 books, with well over 2 million copies in print. Series include **AMERICAN CHILLERS, MICHIGAN CHILLERS, FREDDIE FERNORTNER, FEARLESS FIRST GRADER,** and **THE ADVENTURE CLUB.** He's also co-authored a novel for teens (with Christopher Knight) entitled **PANDEMIA.** When not traveling, Rand lives in northern Michigan with his wife and two dogs. He is also the only author in the world to have a store that sells only his works: **CHILLERMANIA!** is located in Indian River, Michigan. Johnathan Rand is not always at the store, but he has been known to drop by frequently. Find out more at:

www.americanchillers.com

Also by Johnathan Rand:

FUN FACTS ABOUT NEW YORK:

State Capitol: Albany

Became a state in 1777

State Fruit: Apple

State Bird: Bluebird

State Animal: Beaver

State Tree: Sugar Maple

State Fish: Trout

State Flower: Rose

State Motto: Excelsior (means 'ever upward')

The total area of New York is 54,471.144 square miles!

INTERESTING NEW YORK TRIVIA!

☞ The first railroad in America ran between Albany and Schenectady. It was 11 miles in length!

☞ The Catskill Mountains in New York is home to the legendary 'Rip Van Winkle'.

☞ 'Uncle Sam' was originally a meatpacker from Troy, New York. In the war of 1812, he stamped 'U.S. Beef' on his products. Soldiers then began to call him 'Uncle' Sam.

☞ New York has four mountain ranges: Catskill, Adirondack, Shawangunk, and Taconic.

☞ New York was the 11th state admitted to the union.

Don't miss these exciting, action-packed books by Johnathan Rand:

Michigan Chillers:

#1: Mayhem on Mackinac Island
#2: Terror Stalks Traverse City
#3: Poltergeists of Petoskey
#4: Aliens Attack Alpena
#5: Gargoyles of Gaylord
#6: Strange Spirits of St. Ignace
#7: Kreepy Klowns of Kalamazoo
#8: Dinosaurs Destroy Detroit
#9: Sinister Spiders of Saginaw
#10: Mackinaw City Mummies
#11: Great Lakes Ghost Ship
#12: AuSable Alligators
#13: Gruesome Ghouls of Grand Rapids
#14: Bionic Bats of Bay City

Freddie Fernortner, Fearless First Grader:

#1: The Fantastic Flying Bicycle
#2: The Super-Scary Night Thingy
#3: A Haunting We Will Go
#4: Freddie's Dog Walking Service
#5: The Big Box Fort
#6: Mr. Chewy's Big Adventure
#7: The Magical Wading Pool

American Chillers:

#1: The Michigan Mega-Monsters
#2: Ogres of Ohio
#3: Florida Fog Phantoms
#4: New York Ninjas
#5: Terrible Tractors of Texas
#6: Invisible Iguanas of Illinois
#7: Wisconsin Werewolves
#8: Minnesota Mall Mannequins
#9: Iron Insects Invade Indiana
#10: Missouri Madhouse
#11: Poisonous Pythons Paralyze Pennsylvania
#12: Dangerous Dolls of Delaware
#13: Virtual Vampires of Vermont
#14: Creepy Condors of California
#15: Nebraska Nightcrawlers
#16: Alien Androids Assault Arizona
#17: South Carolina Sea Creatures
#18: Washington Wax Museum
#19: North Dakota Night Dragons
#20: Mutant Mammoths of Montana

Adventure Club series:

#1: Ghost in the Graveyard
#2: Ghost in the Grand
#3: The Haunted Schoolhouse

Join the official

AMERICAN

CHILLERS

FAN CLUB!

Visit www.americanchillers.com for details!

Johnathan Rand travels internationally for school visits and book signings! For booking information, call:

1 (231) 238-0338!

www.americanchillers.com

All AudioCraft books are proudly printed, bound, and manufactured in the United States of America, utilizing American resources, labor, and materials.

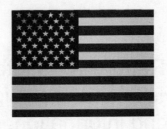

USA